THE DOG HEALERS

A Novel

Mark Winik

ISBN: 1523259434
ISBN 13: 9781523259434
Library of Congress Control Number: 2016900268
CreateSpace Independent Publishing Platform
North Charleston, South Carolina

To all the dogs, who lift our spirits and heal our souls.
Special thanks to the therapy and service dogs.
And closest to my heart, my wife, Norma, and my two dogs, Paco and Chickie.

CHAPTER ONE

"No, stop, please Uncle Freddo, stop!" Isabella cried out. In his inebriated state, Freddo choked the pup by the collar and kept beating him. The helpless creature yelped in pain, and Isabella screamed again for her uncle to stop. She wedged herself between her Uncle Freddo and the dog to stop the beating.

Isabella's mother and brothers heard their cries and rushed outside. The three boys jumped on top of their uncle, but with brute strength, the madman flung them to the ground. Señora Borello's protective instincts left her no option but to react with the closest weapon. She grabbed a wooden two-by-four and slammed Freddo across his head once and then again, dropping him to the ground. While he was down, she rammed him one more time in the groin to make sure he wouldn't get back up.

Isabella sobbed, and her little pup, Echo, shook and whimpered in her arms.

"Mama, Freddo was on top of me and Echo came to protect me." Speechless and filled with anger, Señora Borello held them both close for comfort; the distraught family could take no more.

"Drag your uncle into the barn and set him in the hay," she told the boys. "He's so drunk that he will sleep through the night. And lock the barn door from the outside while you're at it. Your father can deal with his no-good brother when he returns tomorrow."

Señora Borello brought her rattled daughter and the injured pup into the ranch house to tend to their wounds. "I'm sorry, sweetheart. Your Uncle Freddo sometimes loses control. I don't see any serious injuries to either of you, but just to be sure, Enzo will take the truck and pick up the doctor first thing tomorrow morning." She held Isabella and rubbed her forehead, whispering words of assurance. "Mi amore, you and Echo will be fine."

The next morning, the boys were seated at the kitchen table, wolfing down their breakfast. When Señora Borello entered the room, she noticed Isabella's chair was still empty.

"Where is Isabella?"

"She must still be sleeping," Enzo replied.

Señora Borello, panicked by her daughter's absence and sensing something was wrong, ran up to Isabella's bedroom and found the bed empty and made, blankets neatly pulled to the edges of the mattress, and no sign of her daughter or the pup. She shouted frantically downstairs to her sons, "She's gone, let's not waste any time! Go and find her!" The boys scoured the house, opened every closet and cabinet, shook every bush and looked up every tree in the yard, only to return and report that both Isabella and Echo were nowhere to be found.

"Take the horses and keep searching for her," Señora Borello instructed. "She and Echo couldn't have gotten very far."

The three boys took off in different directions, racing their horses over grassy hills, meadows, and wooded patches to the edges of the family ranch in search of their little sister and her best friend, Echo. Enzo pushed his horse hard as he scoured the terrain. Sweat dripped from his temples as he scanned the grass and circled around giant boulders to search for a bundle of girl and dog that could be crouched behind. He thought of his no-good uncle, who more than likely drove the little girl to run and seek refuge in the wilderness. Much younger than the boys, Isabella delighted the family with her love of animals and caring approach to the birds, dogs, and rabbits around the ranch. Isabella and Echo had become inseparable the moment Echo left his mother's litter to join their family. Lost in thought, Enzo almost rode right past a young servant girl on the road. She trudged along silently, kicking up small dust clouds with her soft leather shoes.

"Hola señorita. Pardon me?" Enzo called. The girl turned her face up to him and he recognized her as kitchen help from a nearby ranch. "Oh, it's you. I am looking for my sister, Isabella. You know her, yes?"

"Yes, I saw her earlier near the road, by the woods before the river. A man held her hand; I didn't recognize him, though. Is there a guest at your house? His clothes were very strange. He was tall—very tall. She had a dog, too," the girl said.

"What do you mean? What man? Who is he? I know everyone in this village."

"No, this is a stranger. From a distance he looked a little scary, wearing clothes like a uniform all one color, I think perhaps maroon, a dark deep red, and he was bringing your sister into the woods with the little pup. It was an hour ago, I think. Very early."

"Why didn't you stop them?"

"It's not my business, señor, to stop the señorita."

Enzo gulped and turned from the maid to ride home, not bothering to stop for his horse to drink before pushing the animal into a gallop once again.

<hr />

Banging noises were coming from the barn. Señora Borello ran and opened the barn doors, screaming at her brother-in-law, "My

3

daughter is gone, you bastard, and it's your fault. That's it, we are done. Your brother took you in when you had no place else to go, but now I want you out of here."

"Please forgive me," Freddo implored. "I was drunk last night. Now, what do you mean she ran away? Echo can find her; let him pick up her scent."

"You drunken fool, they're *both* gone. I can't bear the thought of what almost happened, and you nearly killed Echo. If you ever touch my daughter again, I will kill you. Listen closely: The European climb team arrives later today, and if you survive the mountain trek, don't come back. Your brother won't come to your rescue this time."

Señora Borello heard shouts from a distance and the sound of pounding hooves. Enzo appeared out of a cloud of dust and came to an abrupt stop.

"Mother, Mother!"

"Is it Isabella? Did you find her? Is she okay?" Señora Borello demanded.

"Mama, a young girl spotted Isabella carrying Echo and being led into the wilderness by a tall man who was strangely dressed. I can't imagine who it might be and I'm frightened!"

CHAPTER TWO

17 Years Later

My darling wife, Norma, was born in Buenos Aires, Argentina, the tango capital of the world. We visit her family each year along with tourists who flock to Argentina to experience the museums, tango dancers, vineyards, and incredible food.

A great mixture of people emigrated from Italy and Spain, and a smattering from Germany and Eastern Europe, all of whom brought generations of traditions and values to Argentina. Argentineans are world famous for their *asados;* grill masters take pride in serving slow-cooked meats and vegetables. Grilled steaks and aged cheeses are served at perfection and taste like nothing else. Homemade pastas infused with herbed sauces are considered works of art, and the vines of Mendoza produce the finest blends of wines imaginable. Family, food, and wine influence all traditions and provide a festive moment to give thanks and rejoice. This is the soul of Buenos Aires; this is the heart of Argentina.

The city of Buenos Aires brims with nightlife fueled by the Argentineans' boundless energy. Throughout its wide diversity of neighborhoods, the small streets are lined with an abundance of outdoor cafés, a natural place to congregate. You can feel their emotions when the natives speak Spanish, laced with sensuous Italian accents and, of course, the flowing movements from their hands as they engage one another in life. The mild weather and the tempo in the parks give a rhythm of energy or a time to appreciate what we all crave—a moment of peace. But what is truly so special is a warm culture within a large city that loves and welcomes its canine friends.

The locals treat their dogs, and even street dogs, with great respect and lots of affection, an urban society connected to nature and the spirit of their special companions. It is common to be at an outdoor café and have dogs seated beside you, enjoying a special treat while their owners read the newspaper and sip a cup of coffee. Argentineans' great love for dogs is an extension of their warmth and compassion.

Professional dog handlers are commonplace throughout Buenos Aires. It can be a lucrative profession to cater to the tremendous dog population, especially for the upper class, to whom money is no object when it comes to animal care. Packs of mutts and purebreds with wagging tails smile, in numbers that may vary from four to as many as eighteen dogs handled together at once, gracefully moving together in perfect accord.

I was not only captivated but impressed by these professionals, who manage their packs with skilled control, especially when I have a problem walking just one—Bogie, my forty-pound Wheaten Terrier determined to drag me down the sidewalk. I can't tell you how many times he has almost pulled my arm out of its socket. At these moments I'm always embarrassed, but when I look around, I see plenty of dog owners like me, struggling to simply walk their dogs down the street. How do these Argentineans make it look so easy with five, ten, or even eighteen dogs when I can't manage one?

I wanted to learn their secrets, so I watched the professional dog handlers with a careful eye. I soon learned that each morning, hundreds of dog walkers enter the streets with thousands of dogs—a practice for many years. I found doggie daycare in the many parks, a final destination, an oasis in the midst of the city. Canines come with their packs of friends and handlers to hang out, play, tease one another, or just lay still and carefully observe their surroundings. Just beyond these dog packs is a city so vast, bustling with active commerce, tensions from never-ending political protests, historical architecture that brings one back in time, museums that capture the essence of national culture, tango dancing in the streets of San Telmo, fine dining and outdoor cafés that lure the tourists to the affluent neighborhood of Recoleta. Just east is Palermo. Like its sister city in Italy, each block has its own culinary specialty, ranging from traditional Italian cuisine to Argentine grills that capture the carnivore's taste buds with the slow sizzle and the dripping fats of the finest meats in the world. A couple of doors down is Freddo's, known for serving fifty shades of the tastiest naturally flavored ice cream you can imagine. A city filled with endless entertainment, culture, artistic expression, dramatic political corruption, and an extreme difference between the affluent and poor living together: This is Buenos Aires.

Yet I became fascinated with an interesting practice, beyond the eyes of what a normal tourist would see. I soon discovered that many of the dog handlers I'd been watching had been trained in a unique art of massage. This intrigued me and I was determined to see why—and how—this practice seemingly had become so widespread. I hoped to discover something new or useful, perhaps something enlightening, but my immediate challenge was to find a trainer with whom I could communicate.

The dog handlers were everywhere—in the streets, in the parks, and at neighborhood cafés—so I figured it would be fairly easy to connect with one. The first few dog walkers I approached responded with real warmth and great interest, but my Spanish was limited. I decided to go to a larger, busier park, hoping to meet someone who spoke English. It was the Jardín Japonés on the Avenida del Libertador, just across from the Jardín Zoological and Botánico. The park had lush green gardens and peaceful ponds with wooden benches at their edges, which were surrounded by varieties of catalpa elephant ear–looking leaf trees providing adequate shade from the midday sun. After approaching a number of dog handlers, I was able to wrangle some information from a young woman whose English was not much better than my Spanish. Still, she managed to tell me to go to los Bosques de Palermo. It's a magnificent park, and not too far from where we stood. It was there where I was to seek out a man by the name of Carlos DeMarco—the most respected Dog Healer in all of Buenos Aires.

"You can find him in the mornings near the food vendors," she said. "He speaks English," she added.

The next morning, I decided to make this an adventure. I began at one of my favorites in the city, Cafe Martinez, with a cappuccino and croissant. From there, I made my way over to los Bosques de Palermo, picturesque scenes like a postcard, with palm trees, jacarandas sprouting violet flowers, twisting pathways, fish ponds, and lots of picnic areas. Like most of the city's parks on a warm sunny day, it was filled with people of all ages enjoying the simple pleasures it offered. As I walked through this beautiful park, I could feel the energy and the pulse of the people, yet my thoughts of finding Carlos were all-consuming of my purpose.

I was on a mission to find Carlos and his pack of dogs. Los Bosques de Palermo is comparable in size to New York's Central Park and, wouldn't you know, food vendors were everywhere, making my search for Carlos more than a bit challenging. Forget about asking directions to find a dog walker named Carlos—people would just shrug their shoulders or look at me as if I were crazy or, as they say in Spanish, *loco.* I felt like another foolish American tourist, sent on a wild *dog* chase.

After two hours, I was frustrated and about to give up, but as I turned the next bend, I could see in the distance a handsome young man with a pack of eighteen dogs, all different breeds and sizes. Each dog's leash was staked to the ground about five meters apart from the others, enough to give each dog its own territory. This, I hoped, had to be the famous Carlos.

Before I approached him, I decided I would take a seat on a nearby bench and observe him with his dogs. I was pleasured to see the dogs lying still—looking happy, peaceful, and content. Carlos seemed to have the same feeling, lying in the grass enjoying the sun.

After twenty minutes of soaking in the sunlight, Carlos rose and walked over to the most magnificent golden retriever I'd ever laid eyes on. The other dogs lay still and observed his movements. The golden sat attentively as Carlos came closer. In a soft voice, Carlos spoke to the retriever and started to massage his head, slowly moving his fingers around the dog's ears.

I moved a little closer, watching as he continued to work his fingertips up and down the back of the golden. He picked up the pace and applied a bit more pressure, using the palms of his hands as he stood over the dog, whose head was positioned between Carlos's legs. He kneaded the dog's upper thighs, applying just the right amount of pressure, and then pressed his fingertips into the dog's thighs for a few seconds before releasing them.

After five minutes of this exercise, the dog's body still positioned between his legs, Carlos pushed his thumbs into the rear hip area and repeated the same steps, rotating his palms and fingertips. He ended the session with what looked like a scratching technique by running his fingernails briskly across the dog's back, then up to his head, finishing with his ears. Carlos was very precise and focused as he worked hard on the golden. The dog reveled in his touch. Nuzzling into Carlos with gratitude and affection, he must have felt like the luckiest dog in the world.

When they stopped, I approached Carlos and introduced myself to him as Marco from the United States, and expressed how captivated I was to watch him with the dogs.

"Nice to meet you," he said, "my name is Carlos DeMarco, and this wonderful golden's name is Bossa. It is short for Bossa Nova. He comes from a champion line of golden retrievers from Brazil, and his owners believe he should be treated with great respect. So each day I pick him up and he joins the pack," Carlos smiled down at Bossa. "My job is to take care of him, so we walk to the park, we hang out, and I massage him."

"You mean you get paid to massage the dog?" I asked.

"Well, of course. It is considered a respected profession. In fact, I get paid to massage all these dogs."

I nodded, finding it all quite interesting. "Well of course," I said. "It makes perfect sense. If it works for humans, why not dogs?"

I told Carlos that I couldn't help but notice the intensity of his massage techniques and how Bossa appeared to be in heaven as he enjoyed the treatment. He thanked me for the compliment and explained the important benefits of his techniques.

"The dogs love the experience," he explained. "It makes them feel special; it increases their flexibility; improves their circulation; helps them to relax; and perhaps what is most important, it provides the opportunity for a very special connection—for bonding.

"But really, what I do best is teach people an ancient Tibetan art, one that's magical and allows all of us to become Dog Healers. It's a therapeutic exchange that is inherently natural for these animals, and through this process we can experience a sense of rejuvenation and heal ourselves."

I became ever more engaged with Carlos, so passionate the way he viewed human life and the connection with these animals. Finally, he realized that the time had flown by and he needed to return the dogs to their owners. Struck by his wisdom, I wanted to learn more from him and how and where he learned the ways of this ancient Tibetan art.

"Thank you for your time. I would really love to hear more. Perhaps we can continue over a drink later, or even dinner?"

"I'm afraid I cannot make it this evening, but if you would like to join us tomorrow morning, you are welcome to come. I will tell you a story that I am sure you will find compelling and, as many have experienced, one that is life changing."

"I would very much like that," I said eagerly. "What time and where would we meet?"

"Where are you staying?"

I gave him my in-laws' address in Palermo.

"I take care of some dogs that live in that building," he said. "Meet me in front at nine."

We said our goodbyes, and I was excited to spend the next day with him and the dogs. This was not your typical tourist activity, and I couldn't have been more elated by the visions of what the next day would bring.

CHAPTER THREE

I returned to my in-laws' home and was given the traditional greeting of a kiss on one cheek from Norma and from her mother, Matilda. They asked where I had been, and I told them about my adventure, searching for this very special dog walker who is known throughout Buenos Aires.

"This is unique for a tourist," my mother-in-law said, appearing puzzled by what I had just mentioned. "Our city has many beautiful historic districts, museums, interesting shops, and great food, but with all this, you look for a special dog walker."

"Carlos is not just a dog walker," I replied. "In fact, many call him 'the Dog Healer.'"

"Marco, what are you talking about?" asked my wife. "These people are just dog walkers making a living."

"Well yes, this is true, but Carlos is known throughout the city as the man with healing hands."

Both my wife and Matilda rolled their eyes, and Norma asked me, "What do healing hands have to do with dog walking?"

"My new friend Carlos has invited me to go with him tomorrow," I answered. "We'll walk the dogs and he'll teach me his techniques."

"There are so many interesting places to see in Buenos Aires," Matilda fretted, shaking her head. "Why are you choosing to do this?"

"I made a new friend and it's a great opportunity to walk the city with a native and his pack of dogs. It should be a wonderful experience and it's always good to learn something new. Don't you find it fascinating that he's known as the Dog Healer?"

"Everyone else wants to meet our top soccer players or artists—even a corrupt politician would be interesting—but you're captivated by this dog handler," Matilda said, shaking her head again. "Okay, do as you wish, but you must buy this young man Carlos coffee and treat him to lunch."

I nodded in agreement, as a good son-in-law should.

The following day, I rose to the morning mist and was greeted by the bird songs; for me, it meant a special day with Carlos and the dogs. I passed through the steel gates of building security to the streets of Palermo. As I looked to my left, Carlos appeared, strolling with a pack of twelve smiling-faced dogs wagging their tails. The picture of the pack in motion evoked a warm feeling as they walked side by side through Palermo.

Carlos and the pack reached the building and, with extra care, he tied the twelve dogs by one lead to a cast-iron fence, testing his knots twice to be sure they were secure. He then walked over to me and offered a big "Hola" and a hug. "Can you wait with the dogs while I pick up a few more in the building?" he asked.

"Of course," I said. "It would be my pleasure."

A few minutes later he returned with three dogs and a beautiful, elegantly dressed woman who wanted to see her little Yorkie off for the day. Like a mother sending her child to school, she bent down to eye level with her Yorkie, gave it some comforting words, and kissed her baby goodbye.

With impressive skill, Carlos assembled his pack, and off we went through the smaller streets of Palermo with the dogs moving as a team; they did not pull, and they always stopped on his command. We maneuvered through different neighborhoods with little discussion as Carlos focused on controlling the dogs, always mindful of the autos as we crossed the streets.

We came to a city park lined with native artists and vendors selling jewelry, Peruvian knitted goods, handcrafted carvings from Iguazu Falls, and handmade wooden musical instruments. As soon as we found a well-shaded area, Carlos put stakes into the ground to secure the leads; the dogs were panting, and it was time to relax.

I sat in the shade under a tree and waited for him to finish his work and join me. By now I was famished and was glad to see a couple of street-food vendors thirty meters away.

"Amigo, I don't know about you, but I'm starving after our long walk. I'll buy lunch," I said to Carlos.

"Gracias. Just get me something that looks good," Carlos replied.

I ordered an assortment of bite-size empanadas and steak sandwiches for us both, along with a couple of bottles of Agua de La Patagonia, an Argentine favorite with a hint of sweet taste. I asked Carlos about his family life, his friends, his education, and how he became a dog walker. I was especially intrigued to hear about how he earned his reputation. I listened attentively to an astounding story about a special woman named Isabella, who changed his life forever.

CHAPTER FOUR

Carlos was from San Juan, a small town in the western region of Argentina. His birthplace is known for being a highly fertile agricultural area where farmers grow many important crops, including melons, olives, grapes, figs, and a variety of nuts. His father was a farmer and passed away when he was twelve. As the oldest boy, Carlos assumed responsibility for taking care of his mother and two younger sisters.

Carlos proved to be an excellent student who graduated high school with honors, and he was accepted to the University of Buenos Aires. His mother and sisters gave their blessings for him to go, vowing that they would somehow manage to take care of their family farm business.

At the university, Carlos earned both his bachelor's and master's degrees in physical education with a minor in psychology. He became a physical education teacher and coached soccer at a high school in the affluent neighborhood of Recoleta. Life was good for Carlos, and I wondered how a well-educated guy with a great career and a comfortable lifestyle became a dog handler.

It was no time for me to be shy. Would it be rude to ask? I didn't think so. He seemed really proud and happy with his new career, which is more than most people can say. Since diplomacy is not necessarily my strong suit, I took a deep breath and asked him.

"I loved teaching my students and coaching soccer in Buenos Aires," he explained. "But one day I received a call from my mother. She told me my youngest sister, Maria, was ill and that she needed me to help take care of the family farm."

He never counted on having to move back home, but it was his duty. For a handsome single young man, it wasn't an easy transition; being stuck on a country farm was not exactly Carlos's vision of what his life was supposed to be. Nevertheless, it was time to make a sacrifice for the family, and he made the best of his time with his mother and two sisters.

A year passed, and his sister Lucia was accepted to a medical program at the university in Córdoba. Their mother decided it was time for her daughter to get a good education and become a doctor. She gave Lucia her blessing, knowing the family would be well cared for by Carlos.

A couple months later the school session was beginning and, like any good brother, Carlos drove the five hours to take his sister to Córdoba. He decided to spend the night there to help Lucia get settled. The next day he kissed her goodbye and made the leisurely ride back to the family homestead. He drove for several hours, passing through farmlands and forests with a scattering of pine trees, which dressed the rolling hills with shades of green. With his stomach growling and no *parrilla* visible for miles, he pulled over and waved his hands at three traditional-looking gauchos riding toward him on horses.

The gauchos galloped over, thinking that Carlos was lost or had trouble with his vehicle. "Hola, señor, is everything alright?" they inquired.

"Hola, hola, no I am fine. I am taking in the beautiful sights, and to be honest, I am starving and have not seen a place to eat for miles." The gauchos signaled by waving their leather hats for him to follow as they kicked their horses in the side and took off, leaving him in the dust. Up a dirt road, through the mud, Carlos could barely see through the dust created by the horses' hooves as they galloped with lightning speed, but his own wild sense of freedom welcomed this unexpected adventure.

Finally, they came to a rustic ranch house and stopped. The gauchos tied up their horses next to the barn, and Carlos parked his car next to the house. The three gauchos, bursting with the energy of beasts in the wild, introduced themselves to Carlos as the Borello brothers—Enzo, Luis, and Francisco—and welcomed him to the Ranch of Magic Touches.

"You are hungry, mi amigo," the tall, rugged gaucho named Enzo said. "Please join us for lunch and a taste of our family's favorite wine, which, by the way, we make ourselves."

How could Carlos refuse such a warm invitation? Enzo opened a bottle of wine and poured everyone a glass. Francisco—a powerfully built man—stoked a wood fire to prepare their grill, and with a proud smile brought a tray of the finest cuts of *ojo de bife*, rib eye steaks trimmed to perfection, yet marbleized with tributaries of fat, that with the most intoxicating flavor imaginable. Luis, who was smaller in stature than his brothers, but with the same intense dark eyes, walked over with a basket of fresh-picked vegetables from their garden. They sat at a long, distressed wooden plank table next to the house, drank the family's favorite Malbec blend, and had a delectable, hearty lunch. Carlos and the brothers soon became good friends as they exchanged stories. Carlos was fascinated with the gauchos' lifestyle, which consisted of making a living trading and training horses. They lived as though they hadn't a care in the world. How Carlos envied them.

After lunch, and what felt like endless bottles of vino, Enzo joked and said, "We normally have our afternoon siesta, but today we offer to take you for a grand tour of our humble property." They wandered off into the wilderness along a winding trail, and came to a hot, steaming mineral spring. "This is a very special place. The water contains nature's therapeutic minerals, which we use as part of our program for healing horses—and as you might imagine, it serves to soothe the aching joints and muscles of humans as well." Enzo motioned for Carlos to follow. "Please, unless you want to remove your clothes and go for a soak now, I suggest we continue." Carlos followed them down the dirt trail and through a fast-moving mountain brook and approached a row of pine trees that ended at a large fenced-in field. It was a peaceful place, blessed with a scattering of magnificent horses grazing in the grass.

At the far end of the field, a woman on a white stallion was galloping like the wind. She rode around the perimeter, her steed kicking up the dust. Enzo whistled in her direction; she and the stallion flew over a fence with such grace and ease to greet the men.

She dismounted from the horse with a bounce and threw her warm, inviting arms around each of the brothers, and, as was Argentine tradition, gave each a gentle kiss on the cheek.

"Isabella, I want you to meet our new friend, Carlos. We met him on the side of the road near the ranch and invited him to join us for a famous Borello family–style *asado*, accompanied by our sweet homegrown grapes that produce Mendoza Valley's finest Malbec wine." Carlos's eyes glistened as he smiled and stared at the woman in front of him. Isabella leaned toward Carlos and planted her soft lips on his cheek, and with a sweet tone in her voice, said, "It is so nice to meet you."

Isabella was stunning, with long black hair and soft tawny skin—very feminine, yet athletically built. She had a sweet smile, and her large, almond-shaped green eyes shone with pure energy.

"How are things coming along with Tango?" Enzo asked, referring to the stallion she was riding.

"Tango has never been in better shape," Isabella said, with a twinkle in her eyes. "Did you see how we moved around the track and jumped the fence? After Tango's next race, you can rest assured he will be in the winner's circle."

Carlos had never encountered such a woman. She was blessed with natural beauty, and her spirit was alluring. When she smiled, her generous lips parted to reveal dazzling white teeth. It was as if Carlos had been struck by lightning—dazed, but still standing. She simply took his breath away.

"She is a master horse trainer," Enzo told Carlos, "but what's more important, she has a special gift. Isabella communicates with animals through the soft tones of her voice and heals them with the magic that comes from her hands—like no one else in all of Argentina."

Isabella blushed at Enzo's remark.

"She works wonders with horses," continued Enzo, "but dogs are her true passion. You see this horse? He won three major races for all of South America. The most important racehorse owners came from all over to see Tango the champion in action. They were willing to pay big dollars for his stud fees. Sadly for his owner, he got injured, and his spirit was broken and he stopped winning races. He has been through six trainers in the past year and nothing has worked. But Isabella will fix him and bring him back from the doldrums—of that I am quite certain."

Carlos, tongue-tied, was completely taken with Isabella. For the first time, words escaped him. Of course Isabella, being a beautiful woman with keen senses, quickly noticed his state. Enzo, too, had often seen the seductive effect that Isabella had on men, usually proving to be dangerous since she had a history of failed relationships and breaking many hearts. The big, enduring love in her life was that of her animals, especially Malbec, her favorite companion dog. Knowing that Carlos had grown up on a small farm and might still be slightly naïve, he turned to Carlos and attempted to distract him a bit.

"Since we are in such a remote area in the foothills of the Andes, perhaps you are wondering how anyone comes to find the services we offer, and how Tango ended up here."

Indeed, Carlos's curiosity compelled him to ask, "So, how did it happen? Please tell me the story."

CHAPTER FIVE

Enzo looked at his brothers and smiled. He extracted a small cigar from his vest pocket and proceeded to light it, taking his time. He clearly enjoyed the prospect of telling his story. "We work for a small group of wealthy racehorse owners who never share their secrets, especially when they are about horses and trainers. In this particular case, one of our clients asked if we would help one of his business partners in Rio de Janeiro, Ricardo Bennuno, who owned a champion racehorse called Tango. Somehow, Tango had lost his spirit and sustained injuries that were not so evident.

"Ricardo came to visit our ranch and was most impressed with Isabella's skills and unique therapies. He either was a desperate man, or knew what he wanted, so he wasted no time in offering to fly us to Rio de Janeiro. Isabella and I agreed to go, and a couple of weeks later we landed in Rio. Of course, Isabella brought her dog, Malbec. It's sometimes like they are married.

"Ricardo's driver picked us up as soon as we stepped off the plane, and drove us to a private estate just outside the city. A camera identified our car and driver as we passed through the gate.

We drove for a quarter of a mile up to a grand ranch house with beautifully landscaped grounds. The front door opened, and there was Señor Bennuno himself, welcoming us with open arms. 'Hola, hola, it is wonderful to see both of you. I am so looking forward to our new relationship. Please, my ranch is your home,' he said. 'My staff will show you to your rooms. You can rest, freshen up, and we will meet a little later.'

"Shortly after Isabella and I settled ourselves, we gathered on the patio surrounded by exotic plants emitting a perfumed aroma at the rear of the house to break bread. Ricardo poured a fancy bottle of wine into crystal goblets. 'Please, let us toast to our new friendship, and to the making of Tango into a champion racehorse like he once was,' Ricardo said with great vigor. Malbec, lying at Isabella's feet, glanced up momentarily before letting his head sink back into his paws. He approved of the toast."

As Enzo took a last puff on his cigar, he continued with the story. Carlos listened, transfixed.

It was a simple, joyous feast, yet the real focus would be to discuss the new relationship. Ricardo was fixated on the challenge when two young girls with concerned looks on their faces entered the patio, and with them, a lean, muscular brown Lab and a grossly overweight black Lab mix hobbling in behind. Malbec, excited by their presence, wagged his tail and went over to get a good sniff and find out whether these new four legged animals would be friends or foes.

"Papa, the dogs got a whiff of a wild varmint and ran off into the field and they would not come when we called. They just disappeared into the forest. Look, poor Paco is injured." Despite this injury, the Labs greeted their guests with wagging tails; it was no surprise that they gravitated toward Isabella, with lots of licks.

Isabella reached out and received the excited canines with exuberance and affection. She started moving her hands around the dogs' strong bodies, and the moment she stopped, Paco sat before her and lifted his front paw to let Isabella know that he had been injured.

Ricardo watched Isabella work with Paco for a few minutes and said, "I can see that you are not only great with horses; it appears you have a way with dogs as well."

Isabella nodded her head and smiled. Chickie, the other Lab, was sitting next to Paco, staring at Isabella as if to say that she would be patient, but wouldn't stand for Paco's getting all the attention for much longer. Malbec was accustomed to Isabella's connection with animals and looked on with a grin, knowing well the new dogs were receiving something very special.

Adriana, the younger of the two daughters, sensed by the way Isabella touched Paco that she had some training to heal. "Ms. Isabella, he limped and cried the whole way home, and now he has stopped, can you help him?"

"I will be happy to help Paco, provided it will not interfere with my work while I am here." Carla and Adriana gave Isabella a big hug and kiss, realizing that there was something very special about their guest.

That evening, Isabella, Malbec, and Enzo met again with Ricardo and the two girls. As the magenta sun was setting on the distant horizon, brilliant colors beamed onto the patio, and from the east, the full moon rose. The new friends felt the essential power of Mother Nature in their souls as they sipped the sweet liquid from the crushed grapes of their vineyard. They embraced the moment of transition from dusk with mesmerizing colors to a superlative moonlight and beaming stars. Staring into the sky, Ricardo was inspired to reflect on Tango's great moments in horse racing and share them with everyone. "Tango is the most impressive racehorse I have ever owned. He has the power of an elephant and the agility of a leopard, and he moves with the speed of a stallion in the wild. A threat to the horse-racing community, the trainers and jockeys all wished they had such a horse to ride or work with. Like

no other, Tango intuitively knows that when he is on the track competing with a field of champions, his mission is to cross the finish
line first. Yet make no mistake—the champion is the horse to beat,
at any cost. Whether it be on the track or in the barn, saboteurs
will get you if they can. Where there is big money riding on a race,
there is a jockey, a trainer, or a hired hand that will stop at nothing
if given an opportunity. I can tell you some horrific stories, and
who knows what happened to Tango, but let's enjoy the night and
think about the future."

During a candlelight dinner, they discussed what would be a
sensitive approach to meet Tango and engage the confidence of
his trainer and jockey the next day, or, better put, how not to pose
a threat. Carla and Adriana were so enchanted with Isabella and
her feminine approach to this conversation. They wanted to be in-
cluded, and asked if they could come, but Ricardo thought it best
for them to remain home, do their chores, and keep an eye on the
dogs. The girls felt disappointed, and pouted at the thought that
they would be left behind. Isabella knew that feeling, a childish
jealousy of being left out, a feeling that she had often experienced
herself as a young girl.

"Young ladies, why the sad looks? We will check on Paco in
the morning together, and I am going to show you some very special healing techniques that I learned from an esteemed Tibetan
guide. If I recall, I was just about the same age as you when I
learned the secrets of the dog's healing powers, which make them
such special creatures." The girls experienced a swift and sudden
change of behavior, the thought of learning these secrets having
given them an elated feeling of importance. The gifts of a higher
spiritual knowledge were being introduced to their lives, and that
outweighed their thoughts of being left behind.

Next morning, as the adults drank coffee and nibbled freshly
baked chocolate croissants, the girls strolled in with the dogs. Paco
limped over to Isabella and sat down beside her, nudging Malbec

aside. He lifted his paw, and looked at her with beseeching eyes. It meant *Either you feed me some goodies or it is time for my therapy.* So Isabella reached over and rubbed her hands through his coat to locate his pain. Slowly she moved her hands over to his hips and legs and pushed her fingers against his thigh muscle. Paco yelped to let Isabella know where it hurt. She lightly massaged him and whispered something sweet into his ear. Paco responded with a series of licks of appreciation.

The girls looked on with devout attention as Isabella continued with gentle whispers into the dog's ears. This brought warm smiles from the girls and compelled an eager thirst for them to learn and understand what she was communicating to Paco and what Paco was feeling. When they asked, Isabella replied, "I let him know that with each touch, we heal each other." These few spoken words carried so much meaning—the girls would remember them for a lifetime.

Isabella continued to massage Paco's strong, athletic body, and she stretched each of his legs to see how he responded. Paco yelped again as she pulled his left front leg straight out, and Isabella placed her focus on the injured area for a while longer. Ricardo appeared with an anxious look and said abruptly, "I am sorry to interrupt your lessons, my ladies, but we must go before the streets of the city are backed up with intolerable traffic. Girls, give Señora Isabella a hug and a kiss goodbye and we will see you later."

As they navigated Rio's busy streets crowded with pedestrians, they passed farmers bringing their fresh crops to the market on overflowing trucks and donkey carts. In time, the trio arrived at Hipódromo da Gávea, the most popular track in Rio, known for featuring the best racehorses from all over South America. Passing the front of the stadium, they entered through a guarded entrance at the rear, strictly designated for owners, trainers, and jockeys. They parked and made their way through the stalls until they found Tango in number 99.

Tango was housed in a modern stall outfitted with the best amenities. The space measured about 9 meters by 6 meters. One side was Tango's area, and on the other side was an air-conditioned office with a desk, a couple of old wooden stools, and a luxurious leather couch. On the wall was a flat-screen TV. For Tango, there were silver-laden saddles of embossed leather and hand-woven Peruvian blankets that were used for special events.

A few minutes later, Mario, the trainer, arrived with Tango. Tango was a breathtaking white stallion perfectly proportioned, the tone of his muscles rippling with his every movement.

"Mario, I would like you to meet my close friends from Argentina, Enzo and Isabella."

"Pleased to meet you," Mario expressed with some hesitation, unsure as to who these guests were and their purpose for being there.

Enzo and Isabella replied, "It's our honor." They had experienced trainers before that were unwilling to relinquish any relevant information.

"Mario, I would appreciate it if you could share as much information about Tango as possible with them; perhaps they can help us in some way."

Mario responded, "Sure, Señor Bennuno, whatever they need, but may I ask what they're doing here? How can they possibly help me? I mean, really, a *woman* and an Argentine gaucho?"

At that moment, Malbec sensed an evil spirit and grit his teeth and growled at Mario.

"Sorry, I did not mean it. What is wrong with your dog?" Mario asked.

"Nothing is wrong with him, but perhaps there is something about you that he does not like," Isabella replied.

"Please enough of this. They are here to see if they can help Tango and perhaps assist you in some way. Is that not good enough for you?" Ricardo asked.

"Tango is really an extraordinary horse," Mario boasted. "As you can imagine, with any severe injury it can take a considerable amount of time to turn a horse around, yet we are making good progress."

"Can you tell me what you think is wrong with him and how it impacts his performance?" Isabella asked.

"No disrespect, but why do you ask. Are you a veterinarian or a trainer?"

Uncomfortable with Mario's tone, Malbec stood on all fours and warned Mario again.

"Easy boy." She turned to Mario. "We don't quite fit the bill of either of those labels, but surely as you, we have Tango's best interest at heart," Isabella replied.

"Well, he sustained a substantial injury well over a year ago and I have a good track record in rebuilding stamina and performance." Mario replied.

"That is not exactly helping us understand the root of his problem. But maybe I can help further. I have a keen sense for diagnosing," Isabella replied.

"Perhaps you should take him for a ride," Mario suggested.

"Well, it would be nice to take a short walk with him," Isabella replied, "and talk a little. It might help us figure this out. Sometimes these problems are simple to resolve, but they can often be complicated, with more than just one identifiable injury. This could make Tango's recovery slower and more difficult to address."

During their walk around the track, Isabella and Enzo asked an array of questions to help figure things out.

"Mario, would you mind taking Tango for a ride once around the track? Please start with a slow trot and then let him rip into a gallop," Isabella suggested.

Mario mounted Tango and they trotted and then moved into a gallop around the track. As they watched, Enzo and Isabella shared a knowing look, but decided not to say anything. After Mario's ride,

Isabella walked over to Tango, whispered some words of comfort in his ears, and massaged him. Within minutes, Tango responded to Isabella, lifting his head up and down several times—his way of communicating and affirming his acceptance of her, and it was as if he sensed her abilities to help went beyond any trainer's work for the past year.

Tango trusted Isabella and soon gave her free reign to do as she saw fit for him. She combed his body with her hands, pressing her palms and fingertips into his muscles, an exercise that would help Isabella diagnose Tango's injuries. Isabella continued with kneading pressure, and Tango suddenly jolted and signaled to her with a murmur of pain and discomfort. She coerced Tango to lie down on his side and shifted her focus, pressing her elbows into his rear haunches, the area most likely to be at the root of his problems.

After half an hour, Isabella was drenched with perspiration from a deep workout. She embraced Tango, whispered in his ears again: "With each touch we heal each other." Tango nodded his head up and down as he affirmed exactly what she meant. She turned to Mario and thanked him, and motioned to Enzo that it was time to go. As they walked away, Mario internalized his dissent with thoughts of being terminated, heightening to paranoia. His dark side ultimately would seek to ward off anything that threatened his livelihood and reputation.

Ricardo appeared nervous during the ride back to the ranch; he chewed at his cuticles like a man suffering with tense anxieties. He turned to Isabella. "Why are you are so quiet? It's unusual for a woman to not express her feelings and talk. You are making me crazy! Would you mind sharing your prognosis with me?"

Isabella smiled and in a calm manner turned to look at him, her eyes glowing.

"You know, I experienced a very special feeling as I ran my hands up and down Tango's body," Isabella told Ricardo. "It felt as if I were absorbing energy and love from Tango as I pushed my fingertips and palms into his strong frame—the good energy passed through my hands and a warm feeling moved through me."

"Isabella, I don't really understand what you just said," Ricardo replied. "It doesn't have anything to do with my question as to whether you can help or not."

"Señor Bennuno," Isabella said, "even though I spent only a couple of hours diagnosing your horse, we created a connection that will keep Tango and me together for life."

"My dear lady, I consider myself a fairly intelligent man, and I am still not sure what you are saying. Would I understand this better if I were a woman? For crying out loud, can you help?" Ricardo blurted out in frustration.

"I cannot apologize for your lack of understanding, and perhaps you might understand better if you were a woman. What I just experienced with Tango was something magical, and to answer your question—yes, we can help."

"But my dear Isabella, how do you know?"

"I know because Tango led me to his injuries and reciprocated in a way that brought us closer together, but please, señor, I need to speak with Enzo in private before we present you with a work plan."

Ricardo nodded. "Sometimes I think men and women speak a different language, but I do feel something powerful from you, and perhaps this is the feeling Tango is having. Okay! I am eager for us to begin and, oddly enough, I have great confidence in you already."

When they arrived at the ranch, Enzo and Isabella decided to take a walk around the property to discuss something of serious importance.

Isabella turned to Enzo with deep emotion and said, "Enzo, Tango and I connected. We communicated, our spirits embraced, and he showed me the depths of his physical pain. He expressed the sorrow of his spiritual absence, and then he responded to each and every touch from my fingertips. I feel blessed."

"My dear sister, you are truly blessed to feel such passion; you need not say more. Forgive me, but I need to take my siesta. We can discuss our game plan later. I am sure I don't need to tell you that Ricardo is a man with little patience. Now let me hug my favorite sister," he said with a loving smile.

Isabella was not fatigued like Enzo, and she loved the feeling of the warm breeze blowing across her body. She chose to relax in the patio area, with Malbec nearby. Ricardo's girls came with the dogs to join her. Paco, still limping, approached Isabella, sat next to her, and again lifted his injured leg and gazed at her with pained eyes. Malbec caught wind of this and rushed over from the far end of the patio. Paco turned to him, grit his teeth, and growled. It was his way of saying to Malbec, *Nothing doing. Can't you see that it's my time to be treated by Isabella?*

"You know, this one could win an Academy Award," Isabella clucked as she rolled her eyes towards the girls, "and because he is such a great actor he deserves some very special massage therapy, don't you agree?"

The girls giggled, realizing that although Paco was improving, he clearly was smitten with Isabella's whispers and her loving touch.

"He waited on the patio all day for you to return," Carla told Isabella.

Isabella signaled to Paco to come closer and lifted him, placing his front legs on either side of her body as she sat in a chair. She moved her face close to Paco's, and he licked her. She whispered something into his ears and scratched him all over, alternating her pace and force, then continued by feeling his thighs and applying pressure and then releasing her fingertips, again and again, as she moved around his body, always returning to the place of his injury.

Isabella pushed with her palms and then her thumbs into Paco's thigh muscles. After multiple repetitions, she gently lifted

Paco and set him back down in front of her. He looked up at her with adoration; it was symbolic of his deep gratitude. Once again, Isabella had felt this little creature give something special back to her each time she moved her fingers and palms over his body.

After Enzo's midday snooze, he joined them on the patio. The girls greeted Enzo with youthful enthusiasm. "We are so excited about learning Isabella's magic." Enzo assured them that Isabella would soon teach them the magic of her gentle touch and whispers, and the gifts of healing.

"Young ladies, Isabella and I must speak with your father about something of great importance. Would you mind taking the dogs for a walk in the field?" Enzo requested.

When Ricardo joined them, the puzzled look on his face reflected his anxiety and it was obvious that he needed some clarity. Enzo approached him and spoke freely.

"We think that Tango has developed muscle and tendon tension in the upper hip region, which has migrated into the midsection of his legs, thus impacting his racing performance. This is a horse that is accustomed to winning, and we believe his injuries have caused his spirit to deteriorate. His performance can be improved only if we address these issues and correct them," Enzo explained.

"How can this be possible? Mario works hard on Tango's muscle tone and performance and he is considered one of the best trainers in South America."

"With all due respect, Ricardo," interjected Isabella, "Mario may have a good reputation, but frankly, this problem is beyond his scope. He is happy to let you believe Tango will heal in time and take a nice paycheck."

"This is a bold accusation. He has assured me that Tango is coming along just fine and before we know it he will perform like a champion," Ricardo replied.

"I am sorry, but Mario cannot help Tango. He simply does not understand the dynamics of his physical and spiritual pitfalls. We have seen this before. He talks a good game, but he is worthless and it is unlikely that Tango will recover in this environment."

"I find this hard to believe, but does this mean that he will not recover?" asked Ricardo, jolted by Isabella's comment.

"No, that is not what I said at all. I said it is unlikely in this environment. My recommendation is that you have Tango transported to our ranch. I am quite sure that if you give us time to work with him, he will recover and be better than ever."

"But can't you work with him here in Brazil? We can give you everything that you need."

"I'm sorry, but that will not be possible," Isabella replied. "Most male trainers and jockeys do not like to see a woman take their place; their egos cannot accept it. I know from experience that we achieve the best results at our ranch and this is how it must be."

"If this is how it must be, then I will do as you wish. But how much time will it take?" he asked.

"There is no crystal ball for time," Enzo said gently. "Each case is unique and it is difficult to tell you how much time it will take for Tango to heal and return to the winner's circle."

"Well, I am not writing a blank check—it would be nice to give me an estimate," Ricardo answered.

"We typically charge ten thousand per week for a champion racehorse."

"Ten thousand a week!" repeated Ricardo, taken aback. "We are talking big dollars here."

It was a lot of money even for a man of his wealth. If it took five months, the cost would come to two hundred thousand dollars.

"I understand your concern over the cost," Enzo said, "but this is a small price to pay for a champion. That being said, there is no guarantee of anything, so I would like to make an alternative proposition."

"What do you propose?" asked Ricardo.

"Señor Bennuno, we are very confident in our evaluation and our ability to help. I suggest that we devote thirty hours a week to rehabilitate Tango. Our expenses need to be covered, plus a small fee for our time," Enzo outlined. "But for this, we will require a performance contract, which is something that no one else you might work with would request. We have made this exception only once before, and with this type of arrangement, you can stop biting your nails and cease your needless worry about spending money on trainers that show no results. It is our way to express confidence in our ability to truly help Tango."

"What do you mean by a performance contract?"

"A performance contract means that we believe strongly in our ability to rehabilitate Tango both physically and spiritually," Enzo explained. "My best guess is that the process will take from four to six months. We will waive our standard, up-front premium service fee, share the risk, and with your trust, we will also share the rewards. Once we give you the green light, you must guarantee that Tango be entered in the top ten Latin American races for two years. Of course, you will be responsible for the entry fees and transportation expenses. Our proposal is that one hundred percent of his earnings go to us for the first five races, with a fifty percent split of the prize money in the next five."

While Enzo was explaining, Ricardo's eyes had grown wide. "This is a lot of money," he exclaimed. "If we win just three of the big races, that means I will be giving away three million dollars!"

"May I remind you, Tango has performed miserably for the last year, and, if I recall, *you* contacted *us*," Isabella pointed out. "If Tango continues on his current path, he is done, finished, and, I am sorry to say, you will have to retire him at a young age.

"Furthermore, we typically ask for a portion of any stud fees—and I don't mean to insult you, but when was the last time anyone came knocking on your door to breed Tango? Please, Ricardo, surely you can understand that we are assuming the risk, not to mention the loss of time if we are not successful," she continued. "Let's look at the reality of the situation. What have you accomplished in the last year? You have hired and fired six trainers, paid for their services, and have nothing to show for it. Our proposal is not a pipe dream; you know our proven track record. Come on, Ricardo, we're talking about salvaging a most valuable property that you have already invested in heavily. We are offering you hope."

"You had better be as good at fixing my Tango as you are at presenting your case and driving a hard bargain," Ricardo said with a chuckle. "This is a *Godfather*-type of offer." Ricardo sighed. "Okay, you made me an offer I can't refuse, so let's do it."

Enzo and Isabella smiled.

"I like your straightforward style and your confidence, and there's something to be said for dedicating four months of your time," Ricardo said. "I'll have the agreement drawn up as soon as I can."

Enzo and Isabella shook hands with Ricardo, and then Ricardo poured the wine to seal their deal. They made a toast to their new partnership and to great success.

The next morning, the partners met on the patio. The girls came in with Paco and Chickie, and it was no surprise when the dogs went right to Isabella and sat. No commands were necessary; it was Isabella's presence that beckoned them to her side. Once again, Paco lifted his injured leg and gave Isabella his pleading look. Malbec patiently waited, allowing Isabella to bond with another dog.

"Watch us carefully," Isabella said. "I'm leaving for Argentina today, so you girls must learn enough to work on the dogs yourself and help poor Paco heal."

Isabella moved her fingertips up and down Paco's body and then leaned over and whispered in his ear. She took her strong hands and pushed the bottom of her palms, rotating them, into each thigh muscle and then moved her fingertips down the back side, back and forth. She motioned to the girls, asking for their close attention as she focused on Paco's injured front leg, using her palms and fingertips to apply pressure. She repeated this several times, to Paco's delight; the look on his face told the story.

The girls grew excited and impatient. They wanted to show Isabella they were ready to prove their skills. Carla assumed a very serious expression as she went first, massaging Paco—who showed his delight with a wagging tail and a smile from heaven.

That was it for Chickie. She couldn't sit idle while Paco received all the goodies and love. Chickie grit her teeth at Malbec and Paco and lifted her left paw so high in the air it took a great balancing act on her part not to tumble over. The look in her eyes revealed that she too was injured and in desperate need of help. Of course, this was all an act on Chickie's part, but who could blame her? Adriana took care of Chickie while Carla massaged Paco. It seemed that everyone was happy.

The dogs were enjoying every bit of their therapy, and as far as they were concerned, the girls could go on for as long as their fingertips could manage. But it was time for Isabella, Malbec, and Enzo to take their leave. Carla and Adriana gave Isabella a hug and a kiss goodbye.

"Treat both dogs twice a day," Isabella told the girls. "Paco should be fine in a few days. Chickie's a wonderful actress, but how can you blame her—the jealous little girl needs the same love and attention. Please keep in touch and be mindful of the magic of the Dog Healers. You are the guardian angels of these precious creatures, and they will always be by your side and look out for you."

Ricardo kissed each of his daughters goodbye and took Isabella back to the track. Tango needed one final bonding moment and to feel Isabella's touch, smell her scent, and hear the soft warm sounds of her voice before being sent on his journey to the Ranch of Magic Touches.

CHAPTER SIX

Carlos was amazed by the story and began to understand
the background and history of Tango. He was even more
intrigued by what he was learning about this incredible woman,
Isabella.

As Isabella, Enzo, and Carlos walked with Tango through the
woods, they came upon a pool of steaming water. "Why don't you
soak and relax in our hot water mineral spring?" Enzo suggested.
"We call it our Fountain of Eternal Health. It is part of Tango's
therapy, and trust me, Carlos—you will feel like a new hombre."

Isabella approached the spring with Tango. Enzo and Carlos
followed close behind. There was no stopping Tango once he
caught the scent of the pool; he took off like a wild stallion, leap-
ing his way to the middle of the Fountain of Eternal Health.

Carlos couldn't believe what happened next. The sight of
Isabella was more seductive than ever as she slipped out of her
tightly fitting blue jeans and slowly unbuttoned her gauchas shirt
and let it drop to the ground, revealing a pale blue bikini top. She

sashayed toward the steaming pool of water. Carlos was hypnotized by the vision before him.

"Come in for a soak!" she shouted to Carlos from the pool. "It will restore all your vital organs, take your stress away, and the minerals of nature will give you the strength of a young man forever."

Carlos was awakened, but unable to respond. He fantasized for a moment, so alien to him, a scene that only happened in the movies. A sensuous woman had just peeled off her clothes in front of two men, right out in the open. She clearly was not shy; if anything, it was some kind of wonderful flirtatious gesture. All he could do was smile like a boy. He was in awe of her and her wild, free spirit.

Although Enzo disrobed and dashed into the healing spring, Carlos felt boyishly awkward and stood there frozen like a possum, fully dressed, as if fearful of an oncoming predator. Isabella ran out of the water, without inhibition, and moved toward him. Carlos's eyes were drawn to her strong thighs and firm breasts and he was captivated by the water that was now sluicing down her body. Every waltzing step she made revealed even more of her shapely frame and the best of her feminine attributes.

"Come on, don't be shy," she said with a playful smile. "Take off your clothes before I rip them off your body."

Carlos grinned. How could he resist?

"OK, this is something I have never done before. I mean, well, I was not prepared for this," he stammered, "but what the hell, there's a first time for everything. How can I say no to such an invitation" In a flash he had peeled off his clothes and run into the warm spring. Carlos felt free and lighthearted. He did not try to fight any of the religious teachings or beliefs he had grown up with; he just allowed himself to experience the excitement and playful spirit that seemed natural for Isabella. At that moment, she made him feel like the luckiest man alive.

To Carlos's delight, it was more than just the Fountain of Eternal Health; it was a new and exciting chapter in his life. But since all good things eventually must come to an end, it was finally time to head back to the ranch. Isabella returned Tango to the barn and joined the men at the ranch house.

"Please stay for dinner and spend the night," she invited Carlos.

"I would like to," he replied, "but I need to get back to my mother and sister."

Enzo laughed. "What, are you crazy, man? When a beautiful woman extends an invitation such as she has, I suggest you graciously accept, perhaps with words like 'It would be my pleasure.'"

Carlos, bright red in the face with embarrassment, looked at Isabella and said, "I would love to stay. I just need to call home to check on my sister and mother."

"Well?" Enzo said, smiling. "What are you waiting for?"

Carlos picked up the phone and dialed. "Hola, Mama. I just wanted to tell you I met some wonderful people on the way home and I'm going to have dinner and perhaps spend the night at their ranch. Yes, I wanted to let you know and I'll see you tomorrow."

Enzo, the grill master, started a wood charcoal fire for what he boasted would be the finest home-style barbecue ever experienced in all of Argentina, while Francisco came back from the cellar with what he described as the finest Malbec blend in all of Mendoza.

"It comes from our small, humble vineyard."

Suddenly, a clanking sound rumbled through the air as Luis's beat-up truck soon appeared on the dirt-covered driveway, kicking up dust; three smiling dogs had their heads out the window, tongues wagging. Luis brought the truck to an abrupt stop, which produced a minor dust storm. The mud-covered dogs flew out of the truck toward Carlos and greeted him as if he was a long-lost friend.

A few minutes later, Isabella appeared, not in her gaucho-like garments, but in a light, peach-toned linen dress that accentuated her natural beauty. When she approached Carlos, her fresh scent was intoxicating. He could feel his heart pounding.

The dogs greeted Isabella with excitement. She bent over to acknowledge all of them with the touch of her hands; a tender, loving whisper; and a big kiss. There was no question that she was their mistress; she commanded them to sit still and then lie down. Snapping to attention, the dogs complied.

The feast of a lifetime began with wine and empanadas. Enzo shared with Carlos the story of the day that Isabella was smitten by these three lost canine souls, and how she had made up her mind that she and the dogs were meant to be together or, to put it better, the dogs made up her mind for her. Without hesitation, she was compelled to rescue them and bring them home.

"Isabella and I were enjoying a coffee at Sofia's, an outdoor café in Mendoza, when three hungry-looking dogs appeared at the foot of our table—looking for food, love, and a place to call home. Each was more disheveled than the other and they smelled as if they'd been tromping through garbage to feed themselves.

"Despite their unpleasant state, they had keen instincts; the dogs sensed Isabella's kindness, and the rest is history." He gestured to one of the dogs with pride. "You see, this one we call Lola was suffering from an injury when she first arrived. Of course Isabella, the gifted one, nursed her back to health. And this is sweet guy is Malbec. He adores and follows Isabella everywhere, and if you ever had thoughts of a lady being trouble, here is the Conchita. She may be small and sweet looking, but man, she is the queen of instigators. But what can I say, we are one big happy family."

Carlos, clearly puzzled, asked, "Do you mean that you are brother and sister, or are you married?"

"I'm sorry," Isabella apologized. "I thought my brother mentioned this earlier. He loves to play mind games, huh, leading you on to believe that we might be married. This is so typical of just how childish men can be. Enzo and Luis are my brothers and Francisco is a cousin, but he is like a brother. His parents died when he was a child, so we took him in and we treat him as our brother. The three of them seem to think I need protecting—so silly, don't you think?"

Carlos nodded and smiled, surprised but delighted to hear about this small family detail that everyone seemed to be getting a big laugh over. And why wouldn't they, since it was at his expense and not theirs? It was at this moment that Carlos felt the earth shift under his feet and a light shine on his soul. He was aware of something wonderful happening, but did not know he was about to embark on the journey of a lifetime.

After the meal, Isabella offered to take Carlos to the place on the ranch that was closest to her own soul. Through the trees, with the light of the stars and a glowing full moon, they made their way to the top of a bluff. It was enchanting; the moon illuminated the countryside with the most breathtaking views of the valleys as far as the eye could see. With them were three escorts—not the brothers so typical of a protective Argentine family—but rather her three dogs, who stayed by their side, not to protect her alone, but to look out for them both.

"I am kind of surprised and impressed at the same time. It's very unusual for the dogs to take such a liking to a stranger," she said. "They rarely ever let a man get within three meters of me. You know, dogs have keen and clear instincts when it comes to judging people—often they serve as my guiding light, and so far you have managed to pass their tests."

As he crouched down to pet the dogs. "I am honored, but what if I didn't pass their test?"

"They would just rip you to shreds and leave you here for a pack of hungry wolves; by morning you would be nothing more than a pile of bones," she said with a playful smile.

"Better to be devoured by you than by the wolves," Carlos told her, sounding a lot more confident than he felt. He was completely enchanted by Isabella and wanted to kiss her, but was overcome by nerves. He was so close but hadn't the courage to lean over and place his lips on hers.

Not so foreign to Isabella, she liked that he had a shy side. She knew just what Carlos was thinking, and she rather liked the idea, so she decided to make it very easy for him. She turned to the dogs and asked, "What do you think? Is it all right if Carlos kisses me?" The dogs barked once and she turned to Carlos. "That means you can kiss me once and that's all," she said.

It was their first kiss—a passionate one—and certainly one to remember. Even the dogs knew enough to acknowledge it. They howled, and Carlos took this as a sign of their approval. What else could it mean but to share one more kiss? With his eyes shut, he leaned over but Isabella placed her fingers on his lips.

"Their howl means it's time to go," Isabella said firmly.

On their way back, a shooting star pierced the sky and the moon glow cast enough light to help guide them safely back to the ranch house. Isabella showed Carlos his room and kissed him on the cheek. To her surprise, the dogs followed Carlos into his room, having decided that, this night, they would sleep by his side.

At the break of dawn, the heckling sounds of roosters welcomed the day as Isabella and the gauchos prepared themselves for a busy day on the ranch. After a quick breakfast, it was time for Carlos to say goodbye. The brothers expressed sincere pleasure at meeting Carlos, while Isabella and the dogs escorted him to his car. He crouched to the dogs' level and they licked him goodbye. Without asking their permission, Carlos leaned over, embraced Isabella, and placed a second passionate kiss on her lips.

"Carlos, do you have any dogs?" Isabella called out to him as he was leaving.

"Not at the moment," he replied. "But perhaps it would be a good idea for my family to get one."

During his ride home to San Juan, Carlos felt like a young boy experiencing an emotion that most do at one time in their lives—the feeling of romantic love.

When he arrived, his mother and sister were elated to have him home again. Oh, how they had missed him. He told them about Lucia's first day at school and how his ride home had turned into an incredible adventure.

"I met three gauchos on a country road—the Borello brothers—who invited me for lunch and introduced me to their remarkable, lovely sister." Carlos radiated like the sun when he told them. "Isabella is a gifted trainer and has a very special way with horses and dogs. Mama, I had the most wonderful time. The experience has opened up my eyes."

"Carlos, look at you! You're glowing! By the twinkle in your eyes and the smile on your face, it looks to me like you have found love. I am so happy for you, but when are we going to meet this young woman you speak of?" asked Carlos's mother.

"Mama, what are you talking about? How could you possibly know this?"

"Trust me, a mother knows her son. Your father had that same look after he kissed me."

That week, Isabella and Carlos talked on the phone and before long, he invited her to come and visit for a weekend. Isabella graciously accepted his invitation, asking if he liked surprises, and mentioned that she had something special.

When Isabella arrived the next weekend, Carlos and his sister Maria greeted her warmly. "Please let me help you," he said as he reached into the back of the truck and grabbed two bags. As Carlos lifted the bags, a puppy's head popped through the opening of one of them.

"I told you I had a surprise," Isabella said, laughing, as a small, wriggling ball of black and white fluff emerged. She placed the rescued puppy in Maria's arms. Maria beamed. She threw her arms around the dog and thanked Isabella with a hug and kiss. Carlos and Maria's mother was not a big dog lover, but she knew the puppy would bring much-needed joy to the family.

CHAPTER SEVEN

C arlos's mother and sister were intrigued with Isabella's life and her gift for training horses and healing dogs. Their curiosity compelled them to learn of a woman's challenges in a profession completely dominated by men—something unheard of in Argentina.

"I grew up on our family ranch at the foothills of the Andes, just north of Mendoza," Isabella said as she relaxed in a large armchair in the front room. "My father loved the spirit of the wilderness, that each living soul had his respective role in our ecosystem. We were all creatures in the wild, and with time, the evolution of hierarchy transformed, men assuming roles of aggressors or caretakers. He preferred to reside in the civil camp of caretakers and taught me to respect the freedom of the living souls. As a child, I learned to love all creatures; I would spend endless hours in the wilderness and observe the life and actions of any living soul. I would watch the tadpoles evolve and change to frogs for days. The gentle deer and does came to feed in the field, and how quickly they could disappear into the forest for safety to avoid danger from the onslaught of a predator. I would come at sunrise with my dog Echo to our favorite place, Echo's Peak, and we would just lie there. We'd wait and listen for any call in the wild. And with every call, we would cast our eyes on an experience of nature, captivated. I recall many misty mornings; we'd hear the cries of the hawks, the rulers of the skies. They'd glide with ease and survey their terrain, and at any given moment they would suddenly swoop down to the earth or the water with hopes of proudly returning to the skies with prey. I learned all about Mother Nature from my father—the wonders in the wild and the warmth of those who are domesticated. My fascination helped me understand how to communicate with them. It became evident that I had a unique gift.

"My father came from a long line of gauchos, known throughout Mendoza Valley as "the flamboyant cowboys." They would travel for miles to find horses in the wild and tame them; in fact, they started the first rodeo event in the region. My father would share wonderful horse stories passed down through generations. How I loved to sit before him with my legs crossed while he sat in his favorite rocking chair on our front porch, sipping his wine and smoking his favorite cigar. I treasure these memories and all that I have learned about living in harmony with nature and the beauty of the animals. This was one of my father's passions and it seems he has passed it on to me, his only daughter.

"As time passed, he developed a passion for climbing. He had the utmost respect for the great Andes mountains and his love for climbing earned him a reputation as a top guide," she explained. "Climbers from around the world sought out his expertise.

"When I was nine years old, a skilled climbing team came from Europe and set up camp at our ranch for a month as they made preparations for their climb. They contracted my father to help them prepare and guide them up Aconcagua, one of the most treacherous mountains in the world. The winds in the Andes can reach 160 kilometers per hour, and the extreme cold turns the snow on the mountain into a slope of slippery ice. Many climbers have been known to lose fingers and toes due to frostbite. I could never understand what compels these climbers to put their lives in such danger, only to reach a peak at the top and touch the sky. I suppose for those who do not survive, their souls are more blessed, since they are closer to the gates of heaven.

"The climbers that stayed at our ranch proudly represented their countries: two each from Italy, France, Switzerland, England, and Spain. With them came an experienced trek-and-climb crew from Tibet and Nepal in the Himalayan mountain region. This region was known as one of the most difficult terrains for climbing in all of Asia.

"The people who lived in this region were called Sherpas and were well known for their mountaineering expertise. Sherpas were influenced by the monks, who often depended on the them for safe passage, and often rescue. They brought with them these extraordinary animals called llamas, whose job was to carry the supplies and gear on their mountain treks. They also brought with them a unique type of dog. It looked like a cross between a miniature bear and lion. Its coat was light in color and fluffy like a lion, and it had a black tongue. This crossbreed was actually a mixture of chow chow and Tibetan mastiff, and its job was to provide the team safe passage for the dangerous trek. They ran ahead of the climbers, alerting them to any potential hazards. The climbers cherished these animals and fully understood they were of vital importance for such dangerous trips to the top of the world. Even the most skilled teams realized that it could be a journey from which they might never return. Yet their quest to come close to the heavens, for them was something that was so ingrained, they had to try.

"Before the climbers arrived, I met one of the Tibetan guides. He sensed something that had deeply saddened me. I recall that

I was traumatized by something bad that had happened the day before, and I left home. Yet there was something so special about him and his gentle way—I don't know why, but I trusted him, and together we wandered into the wilderness with my pup, Echo. He could feel my pain and noticed my way of dealing with trauma was by connecting with nature. He also sensed that I had a way to connect with the animals.

"His name was Jamyang, which means 'gentle voice' in Tibetan. His job was to take care of the llamas and chowstiffs, but as he put it, 'The llamas and dogs take care of us, for without them, we would not be able to make such a journey. The chows and the llamas rescue our souls from the gates of heaven. We must bless their keen senses, which prompt them to snuggle their warm-blooded furry bodies up beside us and give us warmth and comfort so that we make it through the night, only to awaken to the next day's sunrise and continue our journey, our conquest of the peaks, a place where one discovers a true sense of enlightenment and omnipotence.'

"Jamyang taught me the importance of respecting nature, the beauty in the wild and how the living creatures on earth give us purpose and fulfillment. Still, to this day, I remember his deep connection with the llamas and chowstiffs, and I remember their attentiveness. It was the caring look in their eyes and inner feeling they transcended, a loyal bond with Jamyang. It was deeply moving, so strong and worthy of experience, a connection I desired and yearned to experience and live by for the rest of my life.

"Jamyang had names for all the animals, and called his favorite llama Choden, which means 'one who is devout.' My favorite chow he called Jampah, which means 'loving kindness.' To my delight, Jamyang taught me how I could become a caretaker for all the animals.

"He decided to name me Tenzin, which means 'holder of the teachings.' He said that in Tibet it is customary to give both people and animals names with meaning, for the names represent who we are and project what we do in life. Little did I know at the time that he was preparing me to fulfill an important mission and to follow my inner thirst for knowledge.

"He told me that his mother and grandmother had chosen to call him Jamyang since somehow they knew he would be a spiritual man and that his true mission in life would be as a caretaker for animals. As they had wished, his destined path in life was to work with animals; with a gentle voice and the touch of his hands he would communicate with them. His family nourished his talents and believed that those who practiced a special art of massage and communication could bring magic to their spirits, which enable both animals and humans to heal one another."

Carlos, Maria, and their mother looked at Isabella in wonder. His imagination alight with characters so foreign to Argentina, Carlos implored her to tell them more.

"Still until this day, I have a clear vision of him telling me stories and teaching me about a kind of life that resonated with me. I recall my fascination with the meanings of names and asking Jamyang, 'Why do you call the llama Choden and the chow Jampah?'

"Jamyang replied, 'Both of these animals have many of the same characteristics. Llamas and dogs in particular are extremely loyal. As long as we respect this quality, they will always be there to give us loving kindness. Thus I gave them their respective names.'

"Since I was just nine years of age at the time and a most inquisitive child, I asked, 'Why did you name me Tenzin? I am only a young girl.' Jamyang took my hands and held them for a few minutes, then placed them on Choden and asked me to feel and massage him and speak to him from my heart. Then he took my hands and asked me to massage and scratch Jampah's body and allow myself to receive the beauty of his soul. He then took one of my hands in his and placed the fingertips of his other hand on my lips, then touched my forehead and said, 'You are blessed with a gift. This gift you must cultivate, like a garden, and with this talent and knowledge, teach others what you have been blessed with.'

"Even today I can recall the waves of warmth his touch sent through my body, yet at the time I was not sure what my gift was. And of course, there was nothing in the slightest bit inappropriate in this intimate gesture of his. Jamyang asked me to be patient in the next month and in the years to come; I would learn the essence of my gift and understand its magic and the meaning of my Tibetan name.

"The next month, I spent my days with Jamyang, Choden, and Jampah. We walked across different terrains and mountain streams. The llamas and dogs needed to train and gain strength for the trek, as did the climbing team. Jamyang and I talked about many things in nature and life. We rested three times a day and he observed how I connected with Choden and Jampah.

"He taught me the importance of breathing in different altitudes, about survival in the wilderness, and the importance of stretching and strengthening the muscles. He told me to notice that the first thing the animals do after a rest is to stretch their front legs and then their hind legs. This, he said, would direct fresh blood to the muscles and stimulate an increase in energy; many yoga teachers and their students refer to this technique as the upward dog and the downward dog. I believe the Tibetan masters learned these basic yoga positions by watching the subtle movements of dogs and applying them to their own limbering techniques.

"Jamyang taught me how to communicate with the animals by using a gentle voice. The animals responded as if they knew what I was saying. One thing for sure, they could feel my love for them. I learned to massage the animals and work separately on each muscle group. I learned to apply pressure using my fingers, my thumbs, my palms, and even my elbows, feeling for the muscles that most needed attention. I learned to run my fingers back and forth through their coats, when to be gentle and other times to be strong. Jamyang taught me why this therapy was good for the animals and how it was nurturing for me as well. In Tibet this practice is known as 'Kum Nye.'

"He said that the animals could feel the combination of the touch of my hands and the gentle tones of my voice and it would keep us spiritually connected for life.

"I was curious, and I asked how it could be possible that we would be separated by the ocean and thousands of miles of forests, mountains, and even desert land, and the animals would always feel a bond with me, even after time passed for many years. I could not imagine how this connection could endure the test of time and distance. He said that the bonded spirits in our souls have no boundaries and no meaning in time, that the torch inside us can burn forever and can continue on for generations. The animals and I would always have this connection, no matter where we were, and whether we reconnected in a month or five years later, Jampah and Choden would always remember me, and we would remain spiritually connected. I recall the warm shivering goose bumps all over my body when he conveyed this.

"In time, I began to understand what Jamyang meant. As I focused my energy and applied pulsating finger pressure to Jampah, I could see how he reacted and sensed how it helped him each time. This would always bring a smile to my face and a warm feeling inside.

"The time passed quickly and before we knew it, the month ended. The climbers, Sherpas, and the dogs and llamas were ready to ascend Aconcagua—at 6,961 meters, the highest peak in all of the Americas, and the second highest of the Seven Summits, with only Mount Everest, in Asia, being higher. The climb would take a month.

"I remember the day they started the trek. At sunrise I went to say goodbye to my father and to my new friends-for-life. Jamyang knelt down, held my hands, and said to me, 'Tenzin, you are a great student and, in time, you will apply what you have learned. Because you are a holder of the teachings, many animals and people will benefit from your wisdom. Share your gift with deep passion.

"I will always remember his words, the look in his eyes, and how he touched me inside. I hugged and kissed him goodbye, then I reached over and hugged Choden and Jampah and in a gentle voice said my goodbyes to them. The llama and the chow looked into my eyes and licked me goodbye. I felt a strong bond with them.

"It was time. The climbers and their support team left to begin their trek up the mountain. I remember crying for the next hour, but realized that my tears were not really tears of sadness, but tears of joy. I did not know at the time that my experience with Jamyang and the animals would alter the course of my life. Little did I know how important this knowledge would be for me. Kum Nye got me through the most difficult period in my life."

As Carlos and his mother looked at Isabella in awe, they were speechless, and reflected on the stories and experiences a child could only dream of. Affected by these compelling tales, Maria asked, "What should I name the puppy, Isabella?" She scratched her new friend between the ears.

"It should be a name with strong meaning," Isabella told her. She turned to Carlos. "I hope that one day I can teach you and Maria the same healing technique Jamyang taught me."

Carlos's mother looked on, overjoyed to see Isabella bring new-found purpose to the lives of her daughter and son.

"I promise to be a devoted student," Maria said.

The thought of learning these ancient Tibetan healing techniques was enthralling to Carlos; he had no idea that it would be the start of a new, rewarding career that would change his destiny as well. Isabella's story was like a tale from a novel, but it was a real adventure that captured their imagination. They wanted to know what else might have happened on her journey. They couldn't wait to find out what happened to her father, the European climbing team, and of course, her teachers Jamyang, Choden, and Jampah.

Isabella's eyes glistened with tears; it was something that touched her in a way that she had a difficult time expressing. She looked at the time and said, "This is for another day; it's getting late."

The weekend passed quickly as Isabella skillfully taught Carlos and Maria to handle their new puppy. She expressed how important it was to work with the pup while he was so young. "They are like children that never seem to grow up, but a dog has a strong desire to please you and with good training, and lots of love, your pup will have a wonderful disposition."

Isabella demonstrated the best places to touch and massage the pup. She taught them to communicate using different tones of voice, noting that dogs can often understand what humans say simply from their tone. "In no time you will be speaking dog-talk with squeaky high-pitched sounds that will command their attention as they process the tones of your voice."

Isabella and Carlos spent many weekends together on his farm or at her ranch. Carlos became a great student, and his desire to learn the special massage and scratching techniques were reflected in his performance. The more he learned, the more he wanted to practice on just about any dog he came into contact with. Luckily for Isabella, when he couldn't practice on a dog, she reaped the benefits of his strong, loving hands. It was any woman's dream—a gorgeous man who couldn't keep his hands off her. Their relationship grew, yet it was not without pitfalls. Carlos discovered that as he tried to get closer, Isabella would argue and pull away, and for no apparent reason she would disappear. Enzo had inferred on several occasions that she had a hard time getting close with men in a relationship, that she always seemed to feel more comfortable with furry creatures and found peace in the wilderness. Carlos just kept trying.

CHAPTER EIGHT

Carlos and I were so engaged in conversation that we had nearly forgotten we were in Buenos Aires with his pack of dogs, surrounded by a city of traffic, street vendors, and millions of people. He loved telling his tale as much as I loved to hear it. We had almost forgotten that we had, under our care, twenty dogs that had to be returned to their owners.

The picture was coming together; Carlos learned the healing techniques from Isabella, who had learned from Jamyang. Yet what remained a mystery was how Carlos ended up back in Buenos Aires and what became of him and Isabella.

We quickly gathered the dogs and Carlos skillfully attached each of them to his master lead. While Carlos delivered the dogs, one by one, back to their respective owners, he resumed his captivating tale.

"A few years ago," continued Carlos, "our family's farm experienced a terrible dry spell and our irrigation system failed. It was a difficult time, so I thought it best that we cut our losses and move to Buenos Aires. We sold the farm at a deep discount and moved here. I did everything I could to get back into teaching school and coaching soccer, but there were no positions available.

"Isabella would visit me on weekends, and she noticed all the dog walkers caring for other people's dogs. Coming from a country ranch, she had never imagined dog walkers handling so many dogs at a single time. I remember how excited she became when she experienced the sight of twenty dogs walking together. Buenos Aires was home to a cottage industry flourishing with canine caretakers. It was actually Isabella's idea that I start a dog-care and dog-walking business.

"She convinced me that I could become the most respected dog caretaker and dog walker in all of Buenos Aires. I wondered at first how this could happen. The dog handlers already had their established clients. What could I possibly offer to differentiate my service?

"Isabella's reputation with dogs snowballed throughout South America even as she was earning great respect from racehorse owners. She became known as the guiding light of Dog Healers. Dog lovers, veterinarians, groomers, dog walkers, breeders, and even owners of racing dogs heard about her therapy program. It was only natural for them to want to learn the techniques that Jamyang described in his teachings. The requests poured in.

"I often wondered how all this had gotten started. Her ranch is in a remote area and she was not really exposed to the outside world. Understanding where I ended up and why I am currently in Buenos Aires is possible only by learning the story of how Isabella's life unfolded.

CHAPTER NINE

R icardo became influenced by Mario's constant slanderous remarks about Isabella. It made him grow anxious as several months passed, and Tango and Isabella were still training, with little contact made or updates from her. His frustrations influenced his decision to enter Tango in a second-tier horse race without consulting with her. Despite Tango's improvement, Isabella was never convinced he was ready.

"The two of you are foolish and impatient," Isabella said.

Mario took full advantage of this moment. "I knew all along that Isabella and her new-age healing treatment was just a bunch of spiritual psychodrama. Of course he is not ready, because she knows her business of magic touches and soft tones is just a sham," Mario said.

"How dare you attack me! You don't know anything about me, about what I do and what is good for Tango," Isabella replied.

"Mario, maybe you have been right all along," Ricardo said. "I mean, Tango has been here for three months, she did say he has improved and he should be ready, the men vote to run him in this upcoming race."

"You will regret entering him in this race, and trust me, I will not show my face there," she said angrily.

The race was a disaster. Tango performed terribly and his reputation as a great racehorse was a mere memory. Ashamed, Enzo and Ricardo were ready to throw in the towel, but Isabella soon realized that the severe loss could be favorable for Tango. Everyone now believed Tango would never recover or win another race. The long odds would work to their advantage in that if Tango won his next race—one he was truly prepared to run—the payout could be enormous.

"Look, I warned you not to act prematurely only to satisfy your feeble emotions. Just give me a couple of months," Isabella persuaded the men. "I assure you, Tango will be back at the top of his form."

⚞⚟

For the next couple of months, Isabella and Tango trained with great intensity. She was convinced that Tango was ready—just in time for the Brazilian Derby—and contacted Ricardo.

"Hola, Señor Ricardo," Isabella said.

But before she could get another word out, Ricardo anxiously interrupted. "So you have some good news for me?"

"Si, señor. Tango is perfecto, but please, I want you to come and see for yourself."

"I will fly to Mendoza tomorrow," he said excitedly.

"Bueno, I will let Enzo know, he will meet you at the airport."

Isabella and Tango had worked incredibly hard to build his confidence on every level, but they needed to win more than just the race. They needed to win the respect of Ricardo and the entire racing community. Just as the men drove up she mounted Tango, leaning over to whisper in his ear, "Let's show them what you've got."

Like a true champion, he galloped around the field with swift elegance and grace, before proudly making his way over to greet Ricardo. Isabella hopped off the horse and met Ricardo with a big hug and a kiss.

"We are so happy to see you, Señor Bennuno."

"My dearest Isabella, I owe you an apology. I acted like an impatient, selfish child and since then I've done some serious soul searching. I will never again doubt your words and I really should have known better. A woman's instincts are very keen, and from now on, your word is gospel. So please, tell me, what do you think?" he asked with a stunning grin.

"I have good news and not-so-good news. I will start with the good news. Tango is magnificent; even I, who have worked with the finest stallions in South America, have never been with a horse like him. He rides like the thunder, he moves with rhythm, like a dancer that feels the music, and he acts like he is a champion."

"Wonderful! But please don't tease me. What on earth can the bad news be?"

Isabella couldn't resist teasing him. "Okay, the bad news is that Tango will be the biggest long shot in the history of racing—the odds will be more than 60 to 1."

"But how is this bad news?" he exclaimed.

"Señor Bennuno, I am just playing with you. The fact is, a bet on Tango will return mucho dinero. That is, if anyone dares to place a bet on him."

"You, my dear, can be a real devil, but I am blessed with great fortune to have you on my side. Now, I have some wonderful news for you. The next big event is our Brazilian Derby," Ricardo said with an enthusiastic grin. "I took the liberty of making arrangements already, on a hunch. The rumors have already circulated; they say it will be Tango's last race and the vultures at the track would love nothing better than to put it to me. You should read the editorial in the racing journal. It says, in bold headlines, 'It's Tango's Last Dance with the Stars of the Thoroughbred Community.'"

"Señor, let them think, say, or write whatever they want. My gut tells me the racing community may just be in for a big surprise."

"I hope you're right," Ricardo said.

"The other racehorse owners will be eating their words and their jockeys will get a taste of dirt when Tango leaves them in the dust. In the end, we will be cloaked with the sweetest bouquet of flowers, my partner. But before you go, señor, please walk with us to our field and see how beautifully Tango and I dance together."

The three walked to the field. Isabella mounted the stallion and whispered to him. Tango nodded his head a few times in acknowledgment, kicked up the dust, and galloped with confidence around the track like a champion. Ricardo suddenly recalled a feeling of the past— standing with Tango in the winner's circle. As he imagined this sensation happening again in the near future, it made his day.

A few weeks later, Isabella and Enzo flew to San Pablo for the Brazilian Derby, the most prestigious horse-racing event of the year. They were met at the airport by Ricardo's driver, and went directly to the track to meet with Mario, the trainer, and Luca, the jockey. Mario and Luca seemed anxious about the next day's big race. Enzo couldn't help feeling a little nervous himself, but Isabella was cool and focused. She knew Tango was in much better shape than he had been in a very long time and assured Luca that he would be riding the champion.

That night, Ricardo invited his team to dinner—including his girlfriend, Lucy. Well-spoken, down-to-earth, and a real dog lover, she and Isabella soon found much in common. Lucy specialized in breeding Dogos, a ferocious mastiff-type breed common to Argentina—a dog with a bad reputation and considered an attack dog of the worst kind, feared by most people. Dogos have been known to rip a man's arm off in seconds. Not exactly a pet for the family, but Isabella was curious about the breed, and turned to ask Lucy about them.

"Since I was a child, my love for dogs has been a big part of my life, even greater than my desire to train horses, but why do you choose to breed these Dogos? From what I've heard, they're dangerous animals, so vicious that even a hungry lion would not want to have an encounter with one."

"My Dogos are bred to be gentle giants, not much different from a Newfoundland or a Saint Bernard," Lucy replied. "They're really like any other dogs. Give them a little love and they will grow to be sweet; but if you train them to be killers, they will devour anything that threatens them or their masters. In our case, we give them a whole lot of love from the beginning, socialize them with children and adults, and teach them to love their other furry friends. Sadly, for those bred to be killers, there is little one can do—once a killer, always a killer."

"I ache for domestic animals that never get the love they deserve," Isabella expressed to Lucy as she touched her hand to her heart. "Someday my life will be dedicated to training people to give them the love they truly deserve. Please, if there is anything I can do to help you, let me know."

"Look, the men have finally loosened up a bit," Isabella observed, changing focus. "These guys have been on pins and needles for weeks. I guess there's nothing more important to them than tomorrow's big race."

"A few stiff drinks in their bellies will do it every time," Lucy chuckled.

Isabella rose from the table and addressed the men. "Gentleman, I need to get an early start in the morning and spend some quality time with Tango. Enjoy your evening, but you should really save your fun for tomorrow night. It may well be the most significant victory celebration of your lifetime."

———

Isabella got up at the crack of dawn. She slipped on a pale blue linen dress that clung to her body, accentuating her blessed feminine features, and made her way to the track. The gray mist had settled in around the stadium, making it foggy and cool. She presented her credentials to the guard at the entrance and proceeded to Tango's stall. Tango immediately acknowledged her presence, stomping his hooves into the ground and nodding his head up and down in excitement.

Isabella greeted Tango with affection and he lowered his head and nuzzled his nose on her body. She whispered in his ears and moved her fingertips along his body from head to tail and, with the palms of her hands, she pushed against his muscles and then released. She could feel each breath he took as he relaxed before the big race. He was ready.

In the background, Isabella heard the music and two horns sounding off, signifying that the race was to begin in thirty minutes. Luca and Mario arrived at the stall.

"It's time," Mario said.

Isabella looked Tango in the eyes and touched his nose, giving him the comfort of her confidence. She turned to Luca and Mario and said, "Today is our day and I will see you in the winner's circle."

"We'll give it our best," Luca said.

Isabella hurried back to the suite to join Lucy, Ricardo, and Enzo. She could feel their excitement and tension, and as the odds were displayed on the scoreboard, their anxiety increased. Tango was considered a huge long shot, with odds of 76–1. Calypso came in at 2–1, clearly favored to win. His owner, seated in the box to their right, looked at the odds and couldn't resist commenting. "Hey Ricardo, I can't ever remembering the odds being that bad; well, perhaps once, when someone entered a donkey!" He and his group roared with laughter.

The situation amplified when some wise guy to their left also delivered a nasty comment. "Hey Ricardo, perhaps if you had two female trainers the odds of your donkey would be much better."

Lucy flew out of her seat and threw her drink at the fool who made such demeaning comments. "You are an arrogant, macho jerk! You're lucky my Dogos aren't here; I would have them rip you limb from limb and leave you for the buzzards. You'll be eating your words by the end of the race."

Everyone fell silent as Isabella pulled Lucy down into her seat.

"Wow, you're my kind of girl," Isabella told her. "My emotions were roiling—the curse or blessing of my Italian and Spanish heritage—and I couldn't have expressed them any better. You put that obnoxious creep in his place, and fast. The horse-racing business has been dominated by men forever; it's about time we speak up for our rights. Soon they will learn, and see with their own eyes how the touch from my fingers and the soft tones I use to communicate with Tango are magical. This will be not only a victory for us but for women in horse racing throughout South America."

Suddenly, and without explanation, Isabella excused herself from the suite. She returned just as the one-minute alert sounded. Ricardo's nerves got the best of him as he turned toward Isabella.

"Where the hell have you been? You disappeared. I'm getting a bad feeling and suspect you're not so confident anymore. What's going on?"

"Don't worry, Ricardo," Isabella reassured him, smiling gently. "Today is our day."

"I hope you're right. Now, can you please just sit still? You are making me crazy," Ricardo said as he shifted his focus to Tango's entrance to the track.

His body tightened up like a fully drawn archer's bow as he watched the field being escorted to the starting gates by their trainers. The fans roared with enthusiasm for their favorites. The commentator excited the fans even more as he noted the spectacular moments of each horse and named each mount's jockey. The crowd felt the tension ripple throughout the stadium as the top thoroughbreds in South America were present to claim their trophy. It was hard for Ricardo to imagine victory for Tango.

Once the horses were aligned at the starting gate and the jockeys locked their feet into their stirrups and clung to their horses, they were ready. All eyes were focused on the start with tense anticipation. Tango appeared calm as if he was enjoying the sounds of the trumpets. Poor Ricardo was hunched over, clutching his binoculars, drenched with sweat dripping from his forehead, his crisp white shirt now sopping. He recalled, from Tango's days as champion, that he would be high-spirited and have a look of fierce energy at the gate, but today he was calm. He hoped Isabella's advice to Luca was right, that he save his energy and remain calm before the start. Luca leaned over Tango's head and appeared to be whispering words of confidence into Tango's ear.

As the field of champions settled into the starting gate, the sound of the horn echoed through the stands, and the gates clambered open. The race was underway. Tango came out of the gate well, but after 30 meters he gradually dropped back into the center of the field. As the horses came around the first bend, Tango lagged behind in eleventh position, second to last. Ricardo and Enzo were biting their nails nearly down to the quick. It didn't look good, but at the halfway mark, Tango kicked up the dirt with a burst of energy and started to make his move. By the time they reached the two-thirds mark, Tango had miraculously moved into fourth position. The fans were wild; Ricardo, Lucy, Enzo, and Isabella screamed for Tango.

Coming into the final stretch with vigor, Tango found yet more strength, and like a bolt of lightning, he flashed with ease into second place. As the raging thunder of horses galloped toward the finish line, Tango and the Calypso were neck-and-neck. Then, with a final burst of energy, Tango moved past the favorite by nearly a length as the crowd roared. He had done it. Tango had come through like the champion he still was.

Roaring with joy, Ricardo was infused with energy as he turned to Isabella, launched her into the air, gave her a mammoth hug and kiss, and bellowed, "Tan-go! Tan-go! Tan-go!"

Throughout the stadium, the fans took up the cry: "Tan-go! Tan-go! Tan-go!"

It was the most notorious comeback and upset in the history of Brazilian horse racing. Enzo turned to Ricardo and enveloped him in a bear hug. Lucy and Isabella were a bit more reserved as they embraced. Isabella whispered in Lucy's ear, "I did it." Lucy leaned over and kissed Isabella on each cheek.

Enzo turned to the racehorse owners in the neighboring suites and said, "Hey amigos, not so bad for a donkey; hope you bet on the long shot."

The four walked down to the winner's circle. Isabella held Tango's rein close to her and gave him a big hug and kiss while the photographers snapped shots, their flashes lighting up the winner's circle.

The commissioners and all the dignitaries gathered around to offer their congratulations and present the Derby trophy and the prize money—a check for one million dollars—to Ricardo. Ricardo graciously accepted the trophy and the check and lifted them high above his head. Again he screamed, "Tan-go! Tan-go! Tan-go!" Once more, the fans cheered along with him: "Tan-go! Tan-go! Tan-go!" It was a day for the history books.

⋇

After the ceremony, Isabella decided to take Tango back to his stall and check on his condition. "This is a madhouse," she said to Lucy. "Please, come with us; we need your good company and some peace."

Isabella combed Tango's body with skilled hands. She turned to Luca. "We are a team of champions, and Tango is fine," she declared. Luca was gloating with the victory, but while Mario appeared exuberant, inside he felt disparaged.

"Congratulations," Lucy gave them each a hug and a kiss on the cheek.

"Let's join the men and toast with a glass of champagne," Isabella suggested. Along the way, she turned to Lucy and said, "We just need to stop at the betting window for a moment."

"Well, did you go with your gut?" asked Lucy.

"What do you think?" asked Isabella with a twinkle. "Of course. I never lost faith."

Lucy shrugged. "I have to admit, when I saw the odds before the race, I wasn't as confident, and stayed nervous until the very end."

"I hope you don't mind, but since you gave me full discretion to make a wager as I saw fit," Isabella said, "I bet your $10,000 on Tango to win. And since all things should be equal, I withdrew $10,000 from my operating account with Enzo and put our money on Tango as well. He would have killed me if we'd lost this money."

Lucy beamed. "Well, I don't think he'll be too upset with you when he learns that your bet returned $760,000!" she said.

⊷⊶

That evening, Ricardo took everyone to Luago's Restaurant, a Brazilian Derby tradition, where the winners go to bask in the glow of their victories and the losers come to pay their respects. Luago himself greeted the champion's party, gave his personal congratulations, and escorted them to a private lounge.

Ricardo savored the moment and gladly purchased champagne for all who attended the grand celebration. The establishment was filled with the "who's who" of horse racing; the excitement of Tango's unlikely win had not yet died down. Luago took the lead and spoke into his bullhorn microphone to quiet the room and get their attention. A chorus of spoons tapping champagne flutes helped silence the crowd.

Holding his mic, Luago jumped atop a long wooden table. "Good evening, mis amigos. Today was a race that will be remembered for all time. Luago's is always honored to host this celebration and great tradition. Our Brazilian Derby is the most exciting event in all of South America, and tonight we can honor only one champion. Today we experienced not only a spectacular race, but we witnessed a moment in history—a visual memory that we will always recall,. Moments like these allow us to visualize our dream and give us all hope for tomorrow. Most of us had written off this once-great champion, yet today we celebrate one of the most miraculous comebacks and victories in the history of our continent. I am pleased to introduce Ricardo Bennuno, the proud owner of Tango."

Ricardo walked over to Luago and was lifted by the crowd to join him on top of the winner's table. With a modest smile, he raised his hands to quiet everyone and then asked them to raise their champagne glasses.

"I would like to thank everyone this evening for joining our celebration of Tango's historic comeback and victory. As we all know, Tango had not won a race in two years, and against all predictable odds, this great champion taught us a lesson to be remembered forever in the history of horse racing.

"My heart goes out to all the horses, their owners, the trainers, and jockeys. You have worked so hard to compete in one of the most important races of the year in all of South America, but as you know, at the end of the race there is only one champion. To all the teams and great competitors, I salute each and every one of you, including the horses that put their hearts and souls into this great sport. You are all fierce competitors and this is what drives our passion.

"I would like to bring up my team and introduce the people who have worked so hard to make this comeback possible and put Tango in the winner's circle today. My jockey Luca, who had the courage to stay with us and believed we would come back strong; and Tango's trainer and my good friend, Mario, a man of great dedication and talent who had the fortitude to put us here this evening. I would also like to give my very special thanks to my partners, Enzo and Isabella. Enzo is the consummate Argentine gaucho, who kept our team focused and together. And Isabella is our miracle worker, who healed Tango with her heart and soul, her gifted hands, and an unmatched gift of communication.

"Tonight my friends, my dear friend Isabella will go down in history as Brazil's first female champion racehorse trainer and therapist!"

At that moment, the sound of a horse's hooves pounded the wooden-plank floor in the background. The clatter became more intense as Mario and Tango entered the restaurant dance floor.

The rhythm of Brazilian samba filled the room as they made their way over to Isabella. The guests celebrated the festivity of tradition, while the chant "Tan-go! Tan-go! Tan-go!" echoed through the lounge.

Isabella and Tango danced to the beat of the music. She leaned over and kissed Enzo, Ricardo, and Tango. The photographers lit up the room with their flashbulbs.

"Please, everyone, lift your champagne and toast the finest team I have ever known," Ricardo said as he brought Lucy into the circle. "Today was a great win and I thank the extraordinary members of my team for making this our special day. Salud!"

"Salud!" everyone shouted, clinking glasses. After Isabella dismounted, Ricardo climbed on top of Tango as the photographers snapped more pictures of the winning team for the morning newspapers. Mario then took Tango by the reins, with Ricardo still in the saddle, and paraded him around the restaurant while the patrons offered still more congratulations.

Throughout the night, the other owners came into the private lounge to pay their respects and personally congratulate Ricardo. What they really wanted was to talk to Isabella. So like hawks from the sky seeking their prey, they began to circle her. She was a complete mystery and unknown until this day, so it was no surprise that the losers in the room wanted her magic. Money was no object. They would even overlook the fact that Isabella was a woman, an outsider in the world of horse racing—signifying that the all-men's club had come to an end.

Every owner and agent who came into the lounge left a business card, but according to their agreement with Ricardo, Isabella and Enzo were committed partners for the next five years and could not work with any other racehorses, owners, jockeys, or trainers, whether they wanted to or not. All the same, they enjoyed the attention and felt flattered to be sought after by the most influential people in the world of thoroughbred racing.

The wives of the other racehorse owners also came by to meet them. One in particular, Tamara Comacho, was a big woman, extremely compassionate and down-to-earth. She worked as the director of a South American foundation whose mission focused on a network created to rescue and rehabilitate abandoned and sick dogs. The illustrious ladies made an immediate connection as they recognized a strong place in their hearts for dogs.

Isabella related her own personal experience rescuing three abandoned dogs. Lucy established herself as a dedicated breeder and supported the goals of Tamara's foundation. Tamara lived in Buenos Aires but spent much of her time at the Mendoza Dog Rescue Center, a short drive from Isabella's ranch. By chance, destiny had brought these women together.

The time neared three in the morning, and the festivities began to wind down. The women were ready to go, but just before Lucy and Isabella said their goodbyes, Tamara turned to them and said, "I really enjoyed meeting you and would love for us to get together soon."

"We would love to as well," Isabella responded.

"Let's make it a plan," Lucy agreed.

Isabella and Lucy struggled to get through the drunken crowd to grab Ricardo and Enzo. By this time, the men were slurring their words and could barely stand. As they staggered through the restaurant, the ladies propped them up until they reached their rooms at the hotel.

The next morning, Lucy and Isabella met for breakfast. With the excitement of the Derby behind them, they shifted their focus to envisioning future plans for the Mendoza Dog Rescue Center.

"Perhaps we could use your talents to add a rehabilitation component to the rescue center, and I could use my network and resources to help fund it," said Lucy.

"This horse-racing business is insanity," Isabella said. "Don't get me wrong, I love horses and my dedication and work have brought me to this point in my life. Now it's time I follow my real passion."

Lucy and Isabella shared a smile and felt their deep kinship; they had a new purpose and mission to develop together. The women engaged in intense conversation, losing track of time. There was still no sign of the men, so they decided it was time to return to their suites and drag the men out of bed, throw them under a cold shower, and get them moving.

As Isabella and Lucy passed through the lobby on their way back to their rooms, a group of reporters and cameramen appeared from nowhere and bombarded them with questions and cloyed and pushed for interviews with Isabella. The women weren't aware of the morning's dramatic headlines: Tango had made the front page of every major newspaper. One reporter handed Isabella the *San Pablo Journal*, and there it was, a stunning photo of Isabella and Tango together in the winner's circle, complete with the headline "Mystery Horse Therapist Claims Biggest Victory in Derby History."

The scene evolved into a feeding frenzy. Isabella was a complete enigma and the news people wanted some answers; it was their duty to uncover the mystery and give the public the story of Isabella's life.

One reporter shouted, "Isn't it true that Tango's trainer for the past six months has been Mario Piscatelli, and you are just here for the media story?"

A second reporter chimed in. "Yes, that is what I have heard, that you are trying to take all the glory for Tango's victory!"

The surprise ambush by the press was overwhelming, but Lucy tried to take control of the situation. "Please everyone, Isabella is simply a member of Tango's training team. What's all the fuss? Frankly, her life is dedicated to helping dogs, and the magic of their healing spirits."

The reporters were even more flabbergasted over Lucy's remark, their curiosity growing by the moment. They were screaming one after another to get Isabella's attention.

"What does your work with dogs have to do with racehorses?"

"Where did you learn the skills of your therapy?"

"She has no formal training with horses. This magical healing is just as it appears, it's an illusion, what is known as slight of hand, hocus pocus!" one reporter yelled.

"Can you share the secrets of your magic with us?"

"Why is it that she can't respond to our questions? Something just does not add up here," another accused.

The women tried to make their way out of the crowded circle but were surrounded by media vultures. Just then, Ricardo and Enzo appeared and quickly realized what was happening. The men thrust their bodies forward and pushed their way through the crowd to reach Isabella and Lucy, who were unable to move in any direction. Enzo took their hands and with brisk steps moved away from the press and toward a limousine that was waiting to take them away.

"The news people swarmed us like a flock of lunatics!" Isabella was shouting at Enzo, her voice rising in panic. "Where the hell have you been? It's your job to take care of the press and protect me. You'd better manage these situations in the future—or I'll hire some bodyguards to do it!"

"My dear sister, what can I say but that I am so sorry and it will never happen again. I had a little too much to drink last night, my head feels bigger than a watermelon, and I have a terrible hangover. I won't let this happen again. You're right. I needed to protect you and I should have been there."

Ricardo was unable to address the media and could barely make it through their tight barricade. As soon as everybody was in the limo, Ricardo told the driver to take them to a private landing strip where his plane was waiting to fly them out of San Pablo.

"Never in my lifetime have I seen the press so viciously crazy to get a story," Ricardo declared. "Apparently this is a big one. We're the biggest news story, and not only in horse-racing circles. The story touches the hearts of the people. Young girls can visualize their dreams, but no one knows a damn thing about Isabella. She is in every major paper and on every TV station from here to Mexico." He turned to Isabella. "Like it or not, they've made you famous."

"Look, I didn't sign on for this," Isabella said with an exasperated sigh. "Please, I just want to get back to our ranch. I need some tranquility. Oh no!" she exclaimed as a thought came to her. "What if they know where we live? The last thing we need is relentless paparazzi coming onto the property."

"Don't worry," Lucy said calmly. "Time will pass and with each day the mystery and frenzy will fade, and soon new media revelations will grab them."

As Ricardo stepped out of the limo, he added, "Please, I insist that you wait for the dust to settle and be our guests for as long as you want. My private plane is at your disposal to fly you back to Mendoza whenever you are ready. We'll check with our sources in Mendoza to see what the news is and if there are any reporters snooping around. Until then, mi casa es su casa."

CHAPTER TEN

Enzo managed to calm Isabella, reminding her how much she loved to spend time at Ricardo's ranch. She adored Adriana and Carla, and the girls were thrilled when they returned to the ranch after their hasty departure from San Pablo. Once the dogs got wind of her return, they could not contain their excitement, and charged to greet Isabella, nearly knocking her to the ground.

"Hola to my favorite girls and to your wagging-tailed friends! Listen, I am so happy to see you girls but I am exhausted from the past couple of days. I need to take a siesta and be alone for a while. I promise to spend time with you after I get some rest."

Isabella collapsed on her bed; the experience in Brazil had overwhelmed her. After a few hours of restful sleep, she felt rejuvenated and, as expected, the girls and the dogs were patiently waiting for her. They were excited to demonstrate to Isabella their progress. With a gentle command, the girls had the dogs sit.

Adriana went first and moved her fingers gently up and down Paco's back, and across his head behind the ears. She then pushed her little palms into his muscles. Next, she moved to the big muscles, her thumbs rotating with her palms into the dog's thigh. She ended by giving the dog's back some quick but gentle scratches. Paco smiled with pleasure. When he knew it was over he turned to Adriana and licked her face; it was his way of saying thanks.

Carla took her turn next, using her fingernails to run up and down Chickie's back, as her sister had done. Next, she flipped the dog to the belly-up position and used the palms of her hands in a circular motion across his abdomen. Chickie lay with her four legs stretched and pointed to the sky, smiling.

"I can see you are good students and have learned well," Isabella said, smiling at the girls as she praised them.

"Thank you," Adriana said. "We love it and so do the dogs."

The treatment had become a daily routine. It was a special time that the girls as well as the dogs looked forward to, and in time their bond with one another grew.

"I see a storm front coming from the west. How about we all take a walk around the ranch while we still have some sun?" Lucy said. During their walk, Isabella and Lucy discussed adding a training program in dog therapy to the Mendoza Dog Rescue Center. They knew all too well that the dogs Tamara took in needed much love and attention.

"This therapy program will be the first of its kind," Isabella said. "Educating dog owners is important, still, the dogs' gift for healing us is within them. They need it as much as we do, and the families that come to adopt will leave the center with more than just a companion, but something gratifying."

"Naturally, we can base the training program platform on my therapeutic techniques," she continued. "Once the program is established, it could become a model for other dog rescue centers in Brazil, Argentina, Chile, and Uruguay."

The storm front was moving in quickly and it was time for them to head back to the ranch. That night, they continued with their vision while Enzo and Ricardo continued to celebrate Tango's victory.

"Ha, did you see the look on their faces when I told them, 'Not so bad for a donkey!'" Enzo joked as the two men slammed their glasses, belly-laughing.

"Yeah, 'Hope you bet on the long shot.' Ha, I don't think so! They never expected it, and they deserved what they got, a bouquet of humility and a drink thrown in their faces," Ricardo replied as they continued laughing.

The next morning, Enzo, still feeling a bit hung over, staggered out to the patio. He could hear Ricardo on the phone. "Si, si, I understand. Bueno, thanks for letting me know. Okay, I'll talk to you soon. Goodbye." He hung up the phone with a sigh. "The airport in Mendoza is still mobbed with reporters and camera crews. Perhaps you and Isabella should stay longer. She seemed adamant about avoiding the media at any cost."

"It's very nice of you to offer your hospitality," Enzo said, "but we really must get back to our ranch."

Ricardo nodded. "All right," he said. "Let me see what I can do. I will make a call to another friend, who owns a large vineyard outside Mendoza, not far from your ranch." Ricardo called Daniel back in Mendoza.

"Hola, Daniel, it's Ricardo."

Daniel replied playfully, "What do I owe this honor to? I wasn't sure I would ever hear from a man of great importance such as yourself. Congratulations to you, mi amigo."

"Thank you Daniel, I wish you could have been there; it was truly one of the most monumental experiences in my life. But I need a favor: My trainer Isabella and her brother Enzo need a private landing strip in Mendoza. Can you help us out?"

"For you my friend, I wish I could accommodate you, yet it is a different story for Isabella. She is the pride of Mendoza, and it just so happens that we have a landing strip at our humble vineyard. Just let me know when they will arrive. I will personally greet them with flowers and a case of our finest reserves."

"Muchas gracias. I will let you know their arrival time," Ricardo said, and hung up. He returned to Enzo.

"I have good news! My dear friend Daniel has a private landing strip at his vineyard and he is more than happy to accommodate you and Isabella. I will make plans with the pilot and you can fly out this afternoon."

"This is great news; we really appreciate all you have done for us."

Isabella and the girls said their goodbyes, exchanging hugs and kisses on each cheek. Lucy drove them to meet the pilot.

"I'll be sure to contact Tamara to arrange a meeting so we can discuss our plans for the therapeutic program," Lucy told Isabella.

"Sounds good to me. Thank you for all your help. I don't know what I would have done without you; these men are just plain worthless at times."

Isabella and Enzo boarded the plane and a couple of hours later reached the wine country of Mendoza. A peaceful feeling came over them as they looked out the window; the views of vineyards and olive groves were a welcome sight. The plane touched down on a dirt field laced with nuggets of gravel, as the small plane rattled and bounced endlessly, until it finally stopped. A cloud of dust surrounded the plane, and through the maze of swirling dust, they could see Francisco waving his hands with a big smile across his face.

"Welcome home! Congratulations! My dear sister, you are now a celebrity. Who would ever imagine? Come here and let me give you a hug and kiss."

"I am just happy to see you and be home," sighed Isabella. "The excitement was too much for me to handle. I hope there haven't been any reporters at the ranch."

"You're not exactly out of the woods," cautioned Francisco. "The local news coverage was phenomenal. You're a hero! There was a big celebration, and the people of Mendoza want to congratulate you. I don't know how they got our number, but there have been endless calls to speak with you."

"Listen," Isabella said with annoyance in her voice. "Except for my business with Ricardo, I am finished with racehorses. From now on my life will be dedicated to helping dogs."

Francisco looked puzzled. "Isabella, you're responsible for the biggest comeback in racehorse history. You have all these opportunities, lucrative beyond our wildest dreams, and you want to help dogs—have you gone loco, woman?"

"It's my life, and it's time for me to move on. We made a big hit with Tango by enabling him to win the Brazilian Derby, and fortunately we cashed in, enough for our family. If money is your primary goal, I'm sure Tango will continue to win more races and we will earn more money. But it's time for me to take another path. I'm eager to help dogs and the people they help; we need them in our lives, and we need to be more grateful for all the love they give us. Don't worry. As I said, I will fulfill our agreement with Ricardo. Other than that, you won't find me ever again at the races."

Francisco could see the fire in her eyes, and quickly understood by the rage in her voice that she had made up her mind to choose her own destiny. He was not about to argue with her.

Enzo threw in his support. "We are a family. We are not worried about the money, Isabella. Use your God-given gift to follow your passion. What can I say? We will help you in any way."

CHAPTER ELEVEN

Things quieted down at the ranch, and the family settled back into their daily routine of taking care of the horses and other animals. A couple of weeks passed, and Isabella received a call from Lucy letting her know that she and Tamara were coming from Buenos Aires to Mendoza to spend time at the rescue center and wanted to meet with her. Isabella was overjoyed.

The three women met at Siete Fuegos Asado, a special place where Isabella had rescued her three abandoned dogs, Malbec, Lola, and Conchita. They sat at a round mahogany table shaded by blooming jacaranda trees in the garden patio and sipped their wine while Tamara shared her life story.

She was the youngest of three children; she had an older brother and sister. Her father had earned a law degree, but instead chose to work as an import-export agent and established a network of contracts, which expanded around the globe. Her mother became a successful dentist. Through their hard work and keen insight, the family had acquired a number of valuable properties in Buenos Aires and Mendoza.

When Tamara was eleven years old she was standing on the sidewalk in Buenos Aires on a clear spring day when without any warning, a young driver lost control of his car and struck her. The accident left her with two broken legs, a fractured spine, and torn ligaments in her left shoulder.

"I was really lucky to survive," Tamara said as Isabella and Lucy gave her their full attention. "At the time, the doctors told my mother I would be lucky to walk again. I was confined to a wheelchair for more than a year. My parents had to deal not only the trauma of my injuries, but also with my deep depression. What could be worse for a young girl? I spent most of my days meeting with orthopedic and rehabilitation specialists and felt as if we were just going through the motions. After months of these emotional visits, I saw little improvement and received no hope or encouragement that I would ever walk again." Tamara pulled up her dress and lifted each leg above the table, revealing two large scars on her knees.

"Oh my God, Tamara, you must have been devastated," Isabella said, with Lucy nodding in agreement as tears slowly dripped from her eyes. "The bright side is that you lived to tell us this story and that you can walk again. Sorry, I could not help being so emotional, but please continue."

"After a few months of trying to cope with this family tragedy, my father came home from work and surprised me with the mangiest looking pup, which he had rescued from a shelter. She had long floppy ears and a short snout. She wasn't cute, nor was she ugly, but just funny looking, and frankly, I didn't care how she looked. When my papa placed her on the floor, she took one look at me and flew across room and into my lap. My face was drenched in seconds from her fast slobbering tongue. One after the next, it was like she couldn't get her tongue in or out of her mouth fast enough. She was so excited and it was as if she sensed that she and I were meant to be together."

The ladies smiled with a mixture of sniffles, tears, and joyful laughs.

"Nothing like a sweet loving pup," Lucy said as she wiped her cheeks dry.

"Who couldn't relate to this?" Isabella said.

"Well, honestly, it's those who cannot relate to such an experience that we want to reach out to and touch," Tamara exclaimed with dedication.

"She was just what I needed," Tamara continued. "She brought joy to my life, better than any doctor's medicine. I named my new pup Brassia, after the orchid.

"She *was* like a blooming orchid, like a sweet fragrance. We would fall asleep at night with our bodies and arms joined together. When morning came, she awoke first and felt compelled to lick my face over and over—I guess it was her way of informing me it was time to rise and do stuff together, not to mention that it was time for her to go and do her thing, if you know what I mean. Honestly, she filled my life with joy and gave me hope. Brassia and I were inseparable; she was always by my side, her eyes waiting for my commands, her tail wagging with excitement. I would talk to her and she would give me a look or a little bark—she communicated with me in her own special way."

Isabella and Lucy knew all too well what Tamara meant.

"Although my physical condition limited me, I managed to play ball or Frisbee with her. My mother, whom I always considered clever and a unique problem solver, designed a harness for Brassia and attached it to a custom-made leash. My wheelchair turned into my chariot. Brassia and I were mobile and, for the most part, we could go anywhere together."

"Your father had some keen insight to understand what a difference a dog could make in your life," Lucy said.

"Yes. My father would tell me that I reminded him of the first female gladiator, and that someday I would conquer my fears, and

Brassia and I would run together in the parks and bring freedom to all those who lived in fear of whatever misfortune was cast upon their lives. He made it sound so exciting, and I would try my best to visualize those feats.

"Each day Brassia and I would take the elevator down to the street, accompanied by my mother or father. Brassia pulled me to the park each morning. She helped me get over my fear of being seen in a wheelchair. I remember telling my mother how afraid I was of being ridiculed or looked down upon by other kids. She would remind me that my wheelchair was my chariot, my pen was my sword, and that we would free all who needed to be liberated from their fears and the evil forces of the world."

"Oh my God, Tamara. Such a bad age to go through such an experience," Isabella said. "You must be so grateful for having such loving parents, and that they were keen enough to understand the terror of what this tragedy meant to you. If it's possible to see any beauty in this, it's that Brassia's love for you was so strong and she instinctively knew how to care for you."

"I'm sure Brassia knew how much the walks in the park were helping me. I learned from her to appreciate the small things in life, like the mist in the mornings, sweet fragrance from the flowers, the warmth from sunshine, an afternoon shower, and even a cool breeze. I learned to use and optimize my senses, and my spirits lifted. I looked forward to simple pleasures each day and could feel the world around me in a good, positive light. Brassia was my therapy and she helped heal my emotional scars. Once again I learned to smile; she gave me strength and the hope to move on."

The mystique of a dog's love and its ability to heal humans touched a warm place in their hearts after Isabella and Lucy heard Tamara's story. There was a special connection between dogs and people, one that endures the test of time.

With a faraway look in her eyes, Tamara recalled her days with Brassia. "Each day, we went to the same shaded area and observed all that was around us. Brassia liked to watch the other dogs in the park and I sensed her urge to run off and play with them. She was torn between her sense of loyalty to me and her natural pack instinct to play with other dogs. She deserved at least that much freedom.

"I asked if Brassia could play with the other dogs. My mother thought it was a fine idea and saw no reason why we couldn't try it. She suggested we do it in a fenced-in area and that we ask permission from one of the dog handlers. I watched her play for hours, and each time she returned to my side, her wet dripping tongue hanging out of her little mouth, panting away with a contented smile, I felt her happiness."

Isabella visualized her own three dogs playing together and understood just how Tamara felt as she watched Brassia frolic in the park. What she didn't know was that Tamara's story would take a turn that was similar to when she had found her own dogs—or, more accurately, when they had found her.

"A few weeks later, Brassia was playing with the other dogs in the park, and I couldn't help but notice this husky walking all alone, back and forth, as if he was lost or in search of his master. He appeared frantic with anxiety, and suddenly he just stopped in his tracks and made eye contact with me. Unable to read him, I recall feeling nervous as he stood still, staring me down, when he suddenly charged in my direction and jumped on my lap, nearly knocking both of us from my wheelchair. He began to lick me like a desperate animal in search of some loving affection.

"My mom looked over and said, 'Sweetheart, are you all right? Whose dog is this?' I just looked at her and said, 'I don't have any idea; he doesn't have any name tags, and look at him, he looks like he hasn't been fed for days.' At that point, my mom reached into her bag and pulled out my cheese sandwich and extended her hand with caution. He ravaged my lunch and sat with eyes begging for more. We were both famished and cast our eyes on my mother. 'Okay, I get the picture. I will be back soon so the two of you may feast together,' she said. Moments later, she returned with sliced pieces of steak for my starving friend and a sandwich for me. Together we devoured our food.

"The husky sat by my side and kept tilting his head back, suggesting that we belonged together and that I should take him home. Since he looked as if he was lost or abandoned, I turned to my mother and before I could get the words out, she said, 'I guess I'll have to make another harness, but let's see how Brassia and the husky get along with each other. At first, Brassia was a bit territorial and appeared to be jealous, but the husky was so sweet. He sniffed Brassia and then started to lick her.

"My mother said we could bring the husky home and see how the two dogs were in the house. 'Assuming they are fine together and that your father is okay with it, we can adopt the dog,' she said.

"Back home, the dogs played for hours before dropping from exhaustion, and Brassia's jealousy dissipated. My father arrived and the dogs greeted him with wagging tails.

"Nervous as I was, I recall pleading with my father. 'Papa, the poor pup was all alone and hungry. He really needs our love and a good home. He is really a good guy—just look at how he admires you.' The husky was very smart, sitting attentively with a gazing beg at my father that said, *Please, please señor.* My poor dad didn't have much of a choice and reluctantly agreed, with one condition.

"'First thing we do is give him a good bath,' my father insisted as he stood there clenching his nose from the nasty odor.

"The husky always drank lots of water, so I named him Agua."

"What a wonderful story!" Lucy exclaimed. "Brassia helped you, and you rescued Agua. But please, tell us how your condition changed so dramatically and, thank God, you were able to walk again."

"Over the next few months I continued to see doctors and physical therapists. Although my progress was slow, my spirits changed. I felt liberated— it was my two devoted companions. Even my doctor expressed how I looked different and happier.

"I looked at him with a smile and replied, 'It is my dogs—they are my best therapy.'

"I was so tired from endless doctor's visits. The waiting areas were dark, dreary, and a constant reminder of what depressed me. I prayed each day, I was patient, I wondered when God would go beyond hearing my prayers and act on them. I wanted the use of my legs, to walk in my city and run through the parks with the wind in my hair.

"One evening during dinner, a symbol of hope came. My mother told us that the coach of the national soccer team had gone to her office with agonizing tooth pain. She extracted a tooth that was decayed to the roots, the cause of his suffering. Before he left the office, my mom shared her personal story about my injuries and condition. As a result, the coach insisted that we see the soccer team's orthopedic specialist. If anyone could help, the coach told her, he would be the one. We had an appointment within days.

"I dreaded the thought of one more doctor who would tell me to have patience, that I would heal in time with physical therapy. I sat in the waiting area and prayed for a miracle. After my exam, the specialist brought us in to view the images from their state-of-the-art medical equipment. My mother had a medical background and looked closely as he pointed to the cause of the problem. He told us it would never show up on other X-ray or MRI images, but they have the most advanced imaging system in the country. He said I needed a delicate procedure of reconstructive surgery because the tendons were wrapped tightly around my knees, restricting my ability to walk. He said his favorite player, Vincenzo Lorrico, who had scored more goals than any player that year, had had the same unusual problem. He insisted his personal assistant schedule an appointment for me as soon as possible, because I had suffered long enough.

"My prayers were answered; it was the happiest day of my life since my accident. Two weeks later, I had the operation, and within a few months, I could walk, run, and best of all, kick the ball around with Agua and Brassia. This doctor changed my life, and so did the dogs."

⋯

Over the weekend, the ladies focused their creative energy on the center's therapeutic program. With only limited funds, they needed to raise money and get to work.

"Look at what I had to overcome," Tamara said. "There's nothing that we can't do together."

The three women came to understand one another's strengths and how to best utilize them. Tamara would continue to be their visionary leader; she had hands-on fund-raising experience, having gotten the Mendoza Dog Rescue Center up and running. Lucy would concentrate on development. As a well-respected breeder, she had a network of people whom she could ask for donations. Isabella would develop the training program and instruct the staff. The dogs, of course, inherently knew their role; they would love and touch the spirits of humans as they have always done.

⋯

Two weeks later, Isabella met Lucy and Tamara at the airport and drove them to the Mendoza Dog Rescue Center. Glowing with pride, Tamara gave them a tour of the impressive facility that housed up to one hundred dogs. The spaces for the dogs were like horse stalls, with wooden walls and dirt floors. Along the rear wall was a long pipe with a spigot to deliver fresh drinking water to the dogs on demand.

Behind the stalls was a fenced-in common area where dogs would socialize and exercise a couple of times a day, always with staff keeping a close eye on them. Any dog that displayed aggression would be kept out of this area and away from the others. Dogs with behavioral problems were treated with more individual attention, and would be leash-walked daily by a staff member.

"Hola, hola, and who do we have here?" asked Isabella as two mutts came rushing toward them and jumped with excitement to greet Tamara and Isabella.

"This mixed terrier we call Maestro. He is our resident choir director, who manages to lead the others in melodic howling concerts, while he figures out how to open the gates. No matter how many different ways we have tried to secure the locks, he manages to set the packs free. Isn't that right, Maestro?" Sitting with a sinister yet lovable smile and wagging his tail, he let up a couple of high-pitched howls, proudly affirming that he was guilty as can be.

"But we love him all the same," Tamara said.

"Our veterinarian comes twice a week to examine each dog and provide a health report," Tamara explained. "Over here"—she gestured—"are five special areas for people to spend time with the dog they're considering adopting. We want the experience to be as intimate and memorable as possible, especially for families with children.

"Each week, close to a hundred visitors come. Since we focus on finding good people and good homes, we try to screen all applicants as part of our adoption process. Many get rejected for various reasons. Each dog is certified and leaves here with a good bill of health. Our goal is to nurture the dogs for as long as they need; and we never put a dog to sleep." She turned to Isabella. "I can't tell you how excited we are to add your therapeutic program. It's a dream come true.

"Speaking of a good bill of health, this black Lab is Linguini. She manages to be just the opposite of a good bill of health because she eats not only her meal, but anyone else's she can steal from. A lovable food thief with a good heart and, as you can see, a big stomach. Isn't that right girl?" Tamara said as Linguini wagged her tail in excitement and let out a couple of barks.

Isabella smiled, responding, "As a young girl, I was lucky to learn that my dreams in life could happen. When I was nine years old, a Tibetan healer came into my life. He blessed me with his deep knowledge of healing animals using my hands and the tones of my voice. With each lesson, I learned to treasure how dogs lift our spirits and touch our souls. This is my path; it's my journey and my destiny. Please, help me understand the challenges these dogs may have."

"Sadly," explained Tamara, "The dogs' problems range from malnutrition to aggressive behavior, various health issues, and severe separation anxiety. One thing we know for sure is that most of their ailments can be cured with love and affection, and by placing them in a good home."

As Tamara completed the tour, she led them to a separate building that was used for dogs with extreme aggression problems—a place that could only be considered a detention center for those animals without any hope of solution.

"This will be the future home for our canine rehabilitation facility," Tamara announced.

"Bueno, it needs a lot of work, but it has a warm feeling," Isabella said.

"If it's all right with you, I'd like to have an interior designer give us her opinion," Lucy chimed in. "We need to visualize this, and it certainly helps if patrons and supporters can see with their eyes how it would look."

The women agreed. Although they soon departed, they made a plan to meet at the center again in two weeks. Lucy worked to build a design plan for the center, a strategy to beautify the space, and a plan for construction.

⊷⊹⊷

When the five women convened at the space to share their ideas, they quickly saw that the design had come together.

"Isabella, after giving deep thought to the story you told of the ancient Tibetan treatment, we felt we should honor the traditions and call the rehabilitation facility the Kum Nye Center for Healing." said Lucy.

"That's wonderful, Lucy. The Tibetan healer I spoke of changed my life. It's just now coming to light—the wealth of knowledge and the magic of the techniques that were passed on to me when I was a child. Now it's my turn to pass them on to those who have a great affinity for animals and the wonders of nature." said Isabella.

As they each shared their thoughts and personal stories about the special dogs from their childhoods, Isabella felt the torch light up inside, knowing she had found her life's calling. The memories recounted brought such happiness to the group that if the women had tails, they would all be wagging. Their goals were clear and rewarding: Place dogs in good homes, give every child the opportunity to experience the joy a dog brings, and never forget the needs of the elderly. Simply put, canines make wonderful, loving, and dependable companions.

Lucy was charged with the next phase of the project—raising the $250,000 necessary to upgrade the new building. It would require creativity and hard work. Lucy was charming and knew a lot of wealthy people. Those assets, combined with her strong passion for the work, would help her in her task. Isabella would fine-tune the training program for the center, while Tamara continued to work closely with the group and assist in any way she could.

Tamara and Lucy both worked through their networks to garner contributions. They quickly learned that money was tight, even for people considered wealthy, and that their charm and enthusiasm were not enough. Potential high-net-worth patrons appreciated their vision, but with small donations, a fraction of their anticipated goals. At this pace, the women worried they would never have the funds for the center to open.

CHAPTER TWELVE

They needed a miracle of sorts. Once again, the women met about the fate of the dog center, this time in Buenos Aires. A new perspective was presented, which to some brought doubt, but to others a signal of hope. Tamara had been invited to a fundraiser for children with cancer, and asked the others to join her at the event. It was held at El Ateneo, a historic theater in the heart of the city with high, sculpted ceilings, gilt detailing, and large Doric columns.

The elegantly dressed guests milled around for an hour until the lights dimmed; the room turned dark and transformed the echoes of voices into silence. Florencia Solas, the foundation's director, appeared on the stage, and a spotlight shone on her elegant off-white floor-length gown. She nearly shimmered under the lights. Florencia welcomed her guests and thanked them, in advance, for their support. She eloquently introduced herself and other prominent people in attendance.

"May I please have everyone's attention," she said. "We have a special presentation today, and we hope it touches you the same way it has touched us." Behind her, a large white screen slid down from the ceiling, the spotlight dimmed, and the audience looked up as the video began.

The narrator engaged the crowd with personal stories of children with cancer. The foundation's mission was clear: help lift the spirits of people who needed comfort. The pervasive message was that cancer does not discriminate—rich or poor, young or old—anyone was susceptible. The video concluded with testimony recounting the foundation's success in helping cancer patients and their families deal with the pain and trauma. They hoped to capture the hearts—and pocketbooks—of those attending.

When the video ended and lights again illuminated the space, Florencia made her way across the room to greet the women. "Thank you for coming, señoras. I know that it was never mentioned in our presentation, but I want to tell you just how important dogs have been to the patients in our program. I can't put it into words, but there is something about these animals; it is truly amazing how their presence can light up someone's eyes.

"For a couple of years, a few committed volunteers have come with their dogs and spent time with the patients we reach out to. Although I'm not sure I understand or know how to communicate this, we've noticed that somehow the dogs feel a person's pain. They can sense an illness. They have some inner guide to help a complete stranger. The dogs stay close and have a soothing, almost healing effect. We're so grateful for their unconditional love and ability to brighten up a life.

"They show care and love without a command, without being asked, and with no expectation of getting something in return. I can't tell you how important your group's mission is. I believe from the bottom of my heart that these small, four-legged creatures help us more than we can imagine. I hope that we can explore the synergetic roles of our foundation and your center's work for therapeutic healing," she concluded.

The ladies' eyes lit up at Florencia's comment. Goosebumps ran up and down their arms.

"I would like to learn more about the Mendoza Dog Rescue Center," Florencia continued. "Rumor has it that you're building an amazing therapy facility. From the Mendoza grapevine to the streets of Buenos Aires, I heard that the director of this new program is the leading therapist and trainer in all of South America, and that her work helps more than just dogs in need—it helps people as well."

"Yes, that's me." Isabella nodded, shaking hands with Florencia. "Pleased to meet you."

"I understand they call you the Dog Healer," Florencia said as she looked into Isabella's vibrant green eyes. Isabella, moved by her compliment, offered a shy smile.

"My dear, I have heard wonderful things about you and it is an honor to meet you as well," Florencia said as she and Isabella clasped each other's hands.

"Based on what we've heard today about your foundation, I am without words to describe how much of an honor it is to meet you," Isabella said, "but I hope the warmth and energy from my hands expresses my feelings."

"You know, I am excited. I can see how your program and your dogs will bring some joy to the people we serve. We should meet soon and discuss our visions."

"Oh, I would like that," Isabella said. "We would really like to hear your thoughts." The two exchanged phone numbers, promising to be in touch soon. "Please excuse me," Florencia said. "I must meet the other guests."

Later that week, Florencia called Isabella and invited her to meet her in Buenos Aires on the weekend. "I would love to," Isabella said. " I am meeting my boyfriend on Friday, but I can see you anytime on Saturday." Florencia gave Isabella her address.

"Stop by Saturday morning after nine. We can sit and have some coffee and something sweet."

"I look forward to it."

On Friday, Carlos met Isabella at the airport in Buenos Aires. He embraced her with a warm hug and kiss and presented her with a lovely bouquet of flowers.

"It feels so good to hold you again," Carlos said. "We are going to my favorite restaurant tonight, and tomorrow I am going to take you to a soccer tournament. The best players from South America will be competing and it will be fun for us. It's been some time since we did anything enjoyable together."

"I am sorry, but it's been a long week and I am exhausted. Can we just get a quick bite? And I forgot to tell you that I have other important plans for the weekend," Isabella said.

"You never make time for us. There is always something more important. Perhaps I should have listened closer when Enzo mentioned how you are in relationships. I mean, every time we seem to get closer, you freak out and back off. I am beginning to believe Enzo—the dogs and horses are more important than us," Carlos replied with frustration.

"How dare my brother suggest that! Please, I am tired and I have an early-morning appointment. Let's skip dinner, and you can just take me to a hotel, or I can sleep on the couch at your place. I am not going to let you or my brothers run my life or teach me about relationships."

"I am sorry, I didn't mean to get you upset."

<hr>

On Saturday, Isabella arrived by cab at Florencia's high-rise building in Palermo and was greeted by two guards at the gated entrance. "Buenos días, señora. May I help you?" asked one in a businesslike tone.

"I am here to see Florencia Solas," Isabella announced.

"Oh," said the guard, breaking into a smile. "You must be Isabella." Isabella nodded and smiled back.

"You can wait for Señora Solas in the patio area. We will escort you."

The two guards showed Isabella to the pool and patio area, which felt like an oasis in the midst of the city. The Olympic-size pool was surrounded by well-tended, lush gardens with aromatic jasmine flowers climbing the walls, and towering palm trees. The classic wooden furniture was set on stunning domestic bluestone. Isabella settled into a peaceful feeling, comforted by the ambience, and soon Florencia appeared, dressed in a flower-patterned sundress. They engaged with a warm hug and kissed each other on the cheek.

"My dear Isabella, it is wonderful to see you. I know that we're here to discuss some life-changing moments, but before we begin, I have a secret to share with you—please, from my lips to your ears, only.

"I have known about you for a while now," Florencia said as they each sat down. "In fact, I was at the Brazilian Derby in the suite next to you. My brother and I own the horse named Calypso. As you may recall, he made that obnoxious comment about the donkey and female trainer. I am so embarrassed and owe you an apology. At the finish line, my brother nearly had a coronary; he cursed for weeks at anyone within sight. It was a day he will always remember, but forever wants to forget. Please promise me that you will keep my secret."

Isabella could not imagine what Florencia was about to share. She looked her straight in the eye, held her hands, and said, "I promise to keep this our secret, no matter what."

"Our trainer was close friends with Tango's trainer, Mario. The rumor in the community was that Tango was somewhere in

Argentina undergoing specialized therapy and working with a female trainer. It was a huge insult to Mario. The other trainers in Brazil teased him relentlessly. We heard that the female trainer applied special massage techniques and bathed Tango in hot mineral springs twice a day. We in fact overheard Mario tell some other trainers that you and your brother were just hustlers and were only in this for the money, but I never liked Mario, and to be honest, there is really something shady about him that I could never really put my finger on.

"We were told that you communicated magic with your hands and the whispers of your voice. Although the other trainers and jockeys made fun of you, they still, deep down, considered you a threat. Just before the race began, I followed you up to the betting window. I watched your body language and when it came to the moment of truth, as you placed your bet on Tango, I felt your energy pass through my body."

"Wow, I can't believe that was your brother," Isabella responded. "Lucy was so angry—she really let him have it. I could barely contain myself; he's lucky I didn't lose it as well. I wanted to slap him! But I'm still confused. Why is this a big secret?"

"Well, that's not the big secret," Florencia replied. "The real secret is what took place next. My brother sent me to the window to place a bet on our horse and I did something I had never done before; I went against his wishes, violating a family creed. I took his money and my money, and placed it on Tango to win and boxed it in with our horse, Calypso, for second place. I knew it was extremely risky and the odds for the perfecta were the highest they've been in the history the Brazilian Derby."

"Such a bold move! What made you think Tango would be the winner?" Isabella asked.

"I got such an electrified feeling, a signal, a message from somewhere deep inside of you. I felt the spirit of your confident smile at the betting window when you placed a very sizable wager. I had to go with my instincts. Had my brother known what I did, he would have killed me. How could I bet against the family champion? To this day, I have never been able to tell my brother. In fact, you are the only person I've told. As far as he knows, his bet was lost money. So, my dear, I put my faith in you. Against all odds, I bet the house—we are talking the mother of all bets—on Tango, and I do believe that big thanks from me to you are in order. Please, promise me, this must be our secret. Now, I want to share with you another story that is not public."

"Señora Solas, I am shocked you made this wager," Isabella said. "My brothers would kill me if I ever bet against the family. How could you have taken such a risk?"

"I believed in you and the look in your eyes," Florencia said. "After my brother's nasty remarks, I didn't feel so guilty, and besides, we women must stick together."

"My lips are sealed." Isabella winked.

"What I really need to tell you is that my son, Roberto, was recently diagnosed with cancer. The doctors haven't given us much hope. It's very hard on me and my family, and without much hope, how can we find any joy? I take him for treatments each week, and afterward we spend time in the park. I can't help but imagine the worst scenarios; the darkest thoughts come to haunt me. Nothing could be worse for a mother, feeling so helpless, and when I am alone, I pray every day for a miracle."

"I will pray for you, and for Roberto, too," responded Isabella gently.

"Each day in the park we sit in the shade and watch the dogs play together. This gives both me and my son some pleasure. One day I spoke with a dog walker and asked if he would bring one of his dogs over to be with my son. Since he could see that my son was ill, he was most accommodating. He brought over a sweet terrier, and somehow the dog sensed my son's illness. It was as if he could feel his pain. The pooch hopped up into Roberto's lap and started licking his face. The little terrier made my son feel so special and for that moment in time, we forgot about his illness and simply cherished the moment.

"My son made a special friend and a special connection. Since that day, his spirits have lifted, and no matter what happens, we know this dog has had a positive impact on his life. Such a simple act of love from this animal gave my son deep relief and pleasure. From that moment, I recognized that dogs have a special magic, almost a gift from God, and they have been placed on this earth to fulfill a unique mission."

"I have believed that for a very long time," Isabella said.

"I remember the stories in the news after the Brazilian Derby," Florencia continued. "You were a complete unknown, a mystery to the horse-racing world and to the journalists. With all the rumors about you and Tango's spectacular turnaround, I thought of you not as a horse trainer, but something more. What really stuck in my mind is when Lucy spoke on your behalf and said that you were dedicating your life to helping dogs. Since that day, I've been so curious about you and I am grateful that our paths have now crossed."

Isabella reached out and embraced Florenica's hands. "It's a pleasure. Your work is inspiring, and what you've shared with me reinforces my own commitment."

"I can feel your passion for this work. Giving up a lucrative career with racehorses and dedicating your life to working with dogs is a decision that deserves admiration," Florencia went on. "I feel there's a great need for your wonderful therapy, so I will make you a proposal. We are getting a dog for my son and I would be grateful if you could spend time with Roberto and teach him the concepts of how dogs look out for our well-being. I want him to experience how these wonderful creatures bring joy to us, but more important, I want him to learn how to reciprocate in kind. I hope this will be good medicine, and will help both my son and our family find some welcome moments of joy. Please, Isabella, I implore you. It would be a great favor to my entire family."

"I am honored, and of course I will be there for you and your son," Isabella confirmed.

"Thank you," Florencia said, her eyes brimming with tears. After taking a moment to regain her composure, she asked Isabella, "Please tell me how you learned such special skills."

"I was blessed at an early age; I met a Tibetan healing master named Jamyang. He was a Sherpa mountain guide to some, but for me, he was a guiding light that brought me into the world of understanding the cherished bond we share with animals. He was the caretaker of dogs for the royal family in the mountains of Tibet," Isabella explained. "The palace was guarded by an unusual dog called a chowstiff—a mixture of chow and mastiff. These dogs strategically placed themselves at different locations around the palace grounds during the day, and at night they were trained to sleep with one eye open and use their keen sense of smell to detect any sign of lurking danger.

"For generations, Jamyang's ancestors had passed this gift to their children to heal dogs through special massage and communication techniques. They believed that the dogs needed this therapy on a daily basis. It has remained a great tradition and was their way to show deep appreciation to the dogs for protecting the family and providing them with their unconditional love."

"I have always been fascinated by the Buddhist monks' spiritual insights to life. What a glorious tradition of reciprocal healing," Florencia said. "It was truly a blessing for you to learn this at such a young age."

"I forever hold Jamyang dear to my heart, and I often think of him and long to see him before me again. I will gladly spend time with your son. We can only hope that the bond with his new pup will help in ways that modern medicine can neither understand nor explain. No promises, but I feel certain we'll see some positive effects. His spirits should lift and the stress from the doctor's visits will diminish. He and his pup will have wonderful moments and memories."

Florencia hugged Isabella, tears flowing. "I cannot thank you enough," she said, struggling to get the words out. She wiped her eyes and took a deep breath. "My dear Isabella, there is one more thing I would like to mention. My earnings from the race were substantial, and I am so moved by you—and grateful for your help—that I would personally like to fund the center's project. Yes, one more secret. No one needs to know, including my arrogant brother."

"Thank you! Please, Señora Solas, you can trust in my silence. The funds will come from an anonymous philanthropic dog lover. You and your son will have my unwavering dedication," Isabella assured her new friend.

"Thank you," Florencia said. "We will pick up the pup in a week, and I'd like you to start as soon as you are able. Is that all right with you?"

"I look forward to it," said Isabella.

CHAPTER THIRTEEN

A week later, Florencia toured the rescue center in Mendoza. She carefully observed the available pups and was having such a difficult time making a choice. She wanted all of them. Yet as she walked back and forth, an adorable long-haired male German shepherd caught her eye, and was begging with a repetition of screeching high-pitched barks that seemed to say, "Take me home!"

"Oh my God, look at this ball of fluff. Please let me hold him," she said, signaling to the attendant. The attendant placed the pup in her arms. The excited pup wagged his tail and licked her face over and over. She turned to the attendant and said, "Ah, I almost forgot the fresh smell of a pup and how his soft, furry coat feels so cozy. I guess we have made a mutual decision." As she left the center, she called Isabella to plan her first visit with the new pup and her son. On her way home, she purchased a gift basket, just the right size for the pup's flight home. She lined the basket with a soft, colorful alpaca blanket and placed a couple of squeaky toys inside.

When Florencia arrived home and put the basket down, the fur ball excitedly hopped out and bounded across the room into Roberto's arms.

"My darling, say hello to your new puppy."

As the pup greeted him with licks, a huge smile spread over Roberto's face, and his eyes were glowing. "Mama, I love him! He's the cutest pup I have ever seen." Roberto was overjoyed. He ran to his mother and gave her a heartfelt hug. The pup stayed with him and joined in the excitement, yipping and hopping about at Roberto's feet. "Oh, thank you so much, Mama!" gushed Roberto, his eyes twinkling. "Gracias, gracias, gracias!"

Florencia sighed. Her son's reaction was mirthful and liberating, as if a mountain of worry had been lifted. Roberto and the pup engaged in playful time, without a care in the world, until they both collapsed from exhaustion and snuggled up to each other and slept through the night. At dawn, the puppy's body clock welcomed the sunrise, and he yapped endlessly.

Ah, the great joy of a new pup feverishly barking, Florencia thought. Time to get up, and, by the way, here is a little present for Mama—a fresh unpleasing smell of poop on her ornate oriental carpet. Florencia cleaned up the mess as Roberto and the puppy looked on. She figured this mishap was a small price to pay for seeing her son so happy in spite of his illness, but noted nonetheless to them both, "In the future, Roberto, it's your responsibility to clean or pick up any unwelcome gifts of nature he leaves in the apartment."

"Si, Mama." Roberto could hardly contain himself. "I made a list of twenty names, but I've decided to call my puppy Moisés."

"Moisés is a wonderful name," Florencia told her son. "Today we will get Moisés a collar, leash, name tag, tennis balls, and some toys."

"Yay!" Roberto exclaimed, excited about the day's plans.

"Roberto, where did you come up with the name Moisés?"

"Yesterday, after I made my list of names, I could not make up my mind," Roberto explained. "But I had a dream last night. I was at a camp with other kids. I think they had cancer, too, because some of them were bald. A woman came to visit and she had a puppy with her. Of course, all the kids wanted to be with the pup and, during the day, each kid had a turn. The nice woman taught us to be gentle in how we handled the pup and to pet it with love. She said it would create a special bond between us.

"Mama, the kids loved it, especially when the pup licked them all over. At sunrise the next morning, the little pup went from bunk to bunk, barking like there was something wrong. All the kids got up and the pup ran around in circles. He was communicating with the kids to follow him. So we followed the pup through a dark forest to a small brook and into a field; we were on an incredible adventure. Lots of animals appeared as we moved on our journey. There were giraffes, elephants, hippos, zebras, antelopes, ostriches, and all kinds of strange-looking animals that I had never seen before. The animals were playing in the field, and suddenly the sky opened up with the brightest sun I had ever seen.

"The animals formed a circle around all the kids, and they asked Moisés to lead us into the field of miracles. I woke up and that was the end of my dream. I wish it would have gone on so I could see where the journey took us. I remember the story from Sunday school about the Jewish people, and how Moisés led them through the desert to their promised land; the people kept their faith in Moisés, and their animals followed. This was a miracle.

"Moisés, the pup in my dream, was bringing us to the field of miracles. So I will call my pup Moisés and hope that he will bring us some kind of miracle."

Florencia took Roberto in her arms and kissed him, her tears wetting both their faces. "Sweetheart, I love your dream, and yes, my love, Moisés is your miracle," she said.

"Mama, everyone needs a Moisés," Roberto said as he looked up at his mother.

"My dear, you are so right—everyone needs a Moisés. Now let's go to the park where you and Moisés can play."

⨯

The next morning at sunrise Moisés began the day by barking and barking. Of course, it meant *Time to get up and feed me, and if you don't let me out of here quickly, I will have to lift my leg and stain that lovely rug,* so they threw some clothes on and took him for a walk.

On the way out, Florencia explained to Roberto, "I just want you to know that having a dog is not all fun and games. It means you, my darling, have the honor of assuming a lot of responsibility. You have to walk him, feed him, and clean up after him—then you can have lots of fun together. He will be your best friend forever."

"I understand," Roberto said. But just as they made it to the elevator, Moisés squatted and peed on the floor.

Florencia quickly cleaned up after the pup. "It's all right," she said. "Let's just take him out to see if he needs to do anything more."

This became their routine. Each morning, Moisés needed to be taken outside to do his thing. It seemed like a lot of work, but became a labor of love—and with love comes responsibility. It was making a difference in Roberto's life.

The weekend came and during breakfast, Florencia told Roberto that a very special woman was coming to spend time with him and Moisés. "Her name is Isabella, and she works with young people and dogs. She will teach you to train Moisés. Some people call her the Dog Healer, and you will learn what it means to be a Dog Healer, too."

Roberto's eyes shone with eagerness. "Cool," he said.

"You know, I think you just may be the luckiest boy in all of Argentina. And if you pay attention to Isabella and do as she instructs, you will be the first boy in Buenos Aires to learn these special skills."

"Wow, I can really be the first boy Dog Healer in Buenos Aires," Roberto said, breathless with excitement.

"Yes, but you must be a good student, be patient, and show a great desire to learn."

For the next couple of hours Roberto made it a point to tell Moisés about the guest who would soon arrive. Time passed quickly, and before they knew it, it was midday. The doorman buzzed Florencia and let her know a guest by the name of Isabella was there to visit. "Send her up," Florencia said.

Florencia greeted Isabella warmly and introduced her to Roberto and Moisés.

"Mama says you are going to spend time with me and Moisés to help me train him, and teach us a few things, and if I am a good student, I can be the first boy Dog Healer in all of Buenos Aires."

"It will be my pleasure to help you train little Moisés," Isabella said. "And I look forward to teaching you the art of dog healing. Young man, I have a feeling you will be very good at this. How about we take Moisés for a walk to the park?" she said, while Roberto secured the dog's leash to his collar.

As they walked to the park, Isabella explained the importance of his relationship with Moisés. "It's our job to teach him to respond to our commands. Remember that dogs love to please their masters. From this point on, you must realize that you are his master, and a good master must give his dog lots of love and special talks and touches every day."

Roberto listened attentively; he was excited to learn how to be a good master.

"It looks as if you and Moisés were meant for each other. Walks and playtime in the park are important activities and should become a daily routine. And it's always good to carry a stick; it's like a treasured possession that he will not easily want to relinquish. But a tennis ball is different; dogs love to fetch and return it, for you to throw again and again until your arm falls off. Ah, one more thing: Let's not forget that little Moisés has a healthy appetite. Always pack some treats; we must reward Moisés for his good behavior and for responding to your commands."

"We tried this, but he doesn't always respond, even with a handful of treats," Roberto told Isabella.

Isabella smiled. "Roberto, we don't want to see him get obese. One is enough, and you want him to earn it. When you give him a command, be firm—he will understand the tone of your voice. Treat him with respect and remember that puppies love affection, and they certainly know how to reciprocate with lots of licks. They love to be massaged, so please practice what you learn each day, and you and Moisés will share many great moments together."

Isabella stooped to look more closely at Moisés. "So, Moisés, what do you think about all this?" Moisés gave an enthusiastic bark and wagged his tail.

CHAPTER FOURTEEN

Each weekend Isabella would travel from Mendoza to Palermo to work with Roberto and Moisés. She was accepted and treated like family. Florencia was thrilled by her son's miraculous transformation. He played like a kid should, and his health seemed to be improving.

After a month, Isabella started teaching Roberto the art of Kum Nye healing. Moisés was a healthy pup and had grown about four and a half kilos since her first visit. He was bright, attentive, and affectionate, and the two of them had become inseparable.

"Dogs give us unconditional love, and little Moisés will always be there for you, no matter how you are feeling," Isabella told Roberto. Roberto giggled as Moisés licked his face.

Isabella began the lesson by sharing the story of Jamyang and how his family cared for the dogs of the royal family of Tibet, passing their special massage techniques from one generation to the next. She explained that Jamyang had taught her this ancient art after discovering she had a wonderful way with animals.

"With each touch, the dog experiences the love and affection that provides a feeling of tranquility and spiritual healing for both of you. It is always important to be mindful of how dogs are completely faithful to their masters; they sense when we are sad or injured and need extra attention, and are always eager to help.

"The Tibetan practitioners were keenly aware of the extraordinary bond that humans could have with dogs, and they developed a unique way to give back to them. In time, they were able to see that their massage techniques helped the dogs, and at the same time improved their own lives, both spiritually and physically. From the stories that have been passed down from one Dog Healer to the next, we've learned that if we practice this each day, our own stress levels get absorbed into the air and we feel the love, and our desire to spread it flows like the current of water. They say it is simple magic."

"Magic! Can I do it?" Roberto asked.

Isabella pointed out to Roberto the important muscle groups of Moisés's body. He learned to feel his way around them and pay special attention to the tension in the muscles. He also learned what to do if a dog signals discomfort or pain. She took her fingertips, moving them slowly around Moisés to feel for pain. "It is most important to find the right places," Isabella told Roberto. "All animals have their favorite spots to be touched."

"How will I know if I've found the right place?" asked Roberto.

"Don't worry. Moisés will let you know."

Isabella closed her eyes and began scratching Moisés's head and ears, making her way down his neck and all the way back to the tail. She slowly moved Moisés into various positions that would allow her to be more effective. "You definitely want to make sure that you take care of his legs and thighs," Isabella instructed. "They are the foundation of his strength. Dogs were born to run wild, but for the most part dogs have no place to run in the city. The ones fortunate enough to live on ranches or farms can run free. It's sad that urban and suburban dogs have lost this God-given instinct to run wild and feel free.

"And since Moisés and most dogs live in the city, they need to be walked daily; otherwise they will become fat like a cow. Remember, we are their caretakers and they rely on us to take care of their health. The ancient Tibetan Dog Healers believed that the best medicine was love, through the touch of our fingers. We all have these abilities, and with this technique, we will experience a transformation contributing to our own well-being."

They continued working together, and Roberto learned the best places to apply pressure, how to release, and where to be gentle with his touch. Moisés moved in synchrony with every touch.

"Roberto, place your hand with mine and use your nails and fingertips to scratch little Moisés. Let's discover his favorite places.

"Scratching is important because it reduces stress levels for both the dog and the person. Since Moisés doesn't have the luxury to run free and wild, it's important to improve his circulation with our fingers and palms. This is really critical in his early stages, as it will help him develop into a strong, healthy dog that is bonded to you."

Roberto was proving to be a great student for a young boy. He took his lessons very seriously. "I will massage him every day, and it will help us both be strong," he said.

Florencia listened in on the lesson from another room and smiled, elated by the progress. Roberto was like a new child; it was refreshing, and she was grateful. The other grateful soul was Moisés—each touch was returned with a loving lick.

Moises was growing larger and stronger each week, which raised some concerns over Roberto being able to handle him alone. Florencia needed to find some additional help.

"Isabella, I have some pressing work projects that I must attend to in the coming months, and will need you to spend more time here."

"You know I would love to, but I am afraid I have other commitments during the week. I have someone in mind, though, who I think would be great," Isabella said. "My boyfriend, Carlos. He is reliable, great with dogs, and compassionate with kids and people in general. He recently moved back to Buenos Aires and is one of the few people I've personally trained, so I trust him with my life. I know that you and Roberto will love him."

"Are you sure about him?" Florencia asked. "As you know, I would be entrusting him with the love of my life—my son—and you seem a bit hesitant."

"From time to time we have relationship issues, but he will be great for you, without question," Isabella responded. "I will bring him next weekend and you will see for yourself."

The following weekend Isabella brought Carlos "He is the best dog walker and healer in all of Buenos Aires," Isabella said. "I cannot think of a better person to take care of Moisés and continue to teach Roberto to be a master of dog healing."

Florencia smiled as Roberto walked over to Carlos with a big grin, struggling to lift up the growing puppy. "This is Moisés," he said.

Carlos took Moisés and held him up to his face, looked him in the eye, and said, "This is an exceptional puppy. I can tell someone has been taking good care of him. He is vibrant, friendly—and look at that smile."

"Thanks to Isabella, I learned how to care for Moisés," Roberto said. "Mama says Moisés is a blessing, but I think he is more than a blessing; he's a miracle worker."

"Well, I can see you two make a great team," Carlos said. "How about we all take a walk to the park and spend some time there?"

In the park, Carlos removed a soccer ball from his bag, banged it off his head and kicked it toward Roberto. "Let's see how you kick," he shouted. Moisés instinctively went after the ball and pushed it around with his nose before Roberto could react. Roberto laughed and chased him until their legs could not take it any longer. "It's time to rest now. Let's sit under the tree; it will shade us from the hot sun," Carlos said.

Carlos pulled a bowl and bottle of water from his pack.

"I want to show you what Isabella taught me," Roberto said.

"Sure," Carlos said as Isabella turned on her video camera. "Show me what you have learned."

Roberto closed his eyes and let his fingers navigate up and down Moisés's body, from head to tail, demonstrating his skills with pride.

Isabella zoomed in with the video camera to document the moment for the family library. At home, they played the video. There was a twinkle in Florencia's eyes; she was thrilled to see her son play soccer and practice Kum Nye on his little buddy. After all, it was their therapy.

"What a joy. For a moment I forgot my son has cancer." Florencia smiled as they watched the video to the end. She turned to Carlos. "I would like you to come during the week in the mornings and spend time with my son and Moisés. Since you have been highly recommended and trained by Isabella, this means you are considered the chosen one by two beautiful women—so you must be special."

Carlos laughed and blushed as Isabella reached over and ruffled his hair.

"I will pay you handsomely, and if things go well, there will be greater rewards for you in the near future," Florencia told Carlos.

CHAPTER FIFTEEN

Carlos was happy to work for Señora Solas. He found that not only was she dynamic, but his greatest reward was to witness the joy of the relationship the dog and the boy shared.

He spent the next few weeks traveling to the home of Roberto and Moisés. Each day was the same, so to keep life more interesting, Carlos turned the training sessions into an adventure by exploring different areas of the park. The trio set up camp in a new place each day and recorded each new location, careful to document their progress with video for the rescue center's library. Isabella joined on weekends. Carlos loved so many things about her and felt the same from her, but often she would get close and then she would inexplicably push him away. He could never quite put his finger on it. Carlos asked his mother, the only woman he felt comfortable enough to share his relationship troubles with, for advice.

"Mama, I care about Isabella very deeply, but sometimes she just freaks out and I don't know why. The closer I try to get, the more she pulls away. Why do women do this?"

"Well, she seems like a wonderful person, but I got the sense there was quite a past to that girl. You will just have to be patient with her, I think, if she means that much to you."

"But what can I do about it right now?"

"Like I said, patience, my dear. I know you miss her when she is away, but perhaps it is better that she works at the rescue center or the family ranch during the week. In time, she'll work it out."

⋙✝✝⋘

As the weeks passed, Roberto showed signs of improvement in more than just his spirit. He was improving physically and getting stronger. His appetite was healthy, his cheeks were pink, and he was full of energy and life. Each day seemed blessed like a miracle. Florencia and Isabella believed that it was a combination of the medical treatment and the love Roberto and Moisés shared.

The doctors were mystified by his improved condition, but based on his progress, they made a decision to halt Roberto's treatment for the time being.

Florencia was more convinced than ever of the synergistic connection that her cancer foundation could have with therapy dogs as true healers. This experience gave her a new outlook and purpose, one that was more powerful than the medicine—it was the power of healing the spirit with a special kind of love, and she wanted the spirit healers to help others.

"Please, Florencia, join us next weekend; we can use your help developing the Kum Nye Center for Healing," Isabella suggested.

"I would be honored to, and I will give you all the support I can," Florencia said as she handed over a pale green envelope with a pink bow attached. "Please take this anonymous philanthropic donation as a token of my utmost appreciation."

"Thank you so much," Isabella said as she took the envelope from Florencia. "I know you would be a great asset to the group."

Soon Isabella introduced Carlos and Florencia to Tamara and Lucy. The two were natural additions to the mission and progress of the healing center.

CHAPTER SIXTEEN

During the next couple of months, Isabella and Carlos learned to appreciate the dedicated volunteers who cared for the dogs. They selected a few to whom they would teach the basics of Kum Nye healing. The concept of reciprocation and mutual healing invoked a sense of pride with the volunteers, who were clamoring to learn. Even the dogs that lived at the shelter, patiently waiting for a new home, showed signs of a desire to participate. Isabella and Carlos began to offer hands-on workshops to meet the growing demand.

Twenty volunteers of all ages attended the first workshop. Carlos and Isabella divided them into two groups. The workshops ran three hours in the morning and another three in the afternoon.

The lessons began with the center's mission and focused on explaining how humans and dogs communicated with each other.

"When you learn the teachings of Kum Nye healing, both you and the dog will experience a bond that stays within in both of you. Please close your eyes, feel the energy in your fingertips. Feel your dog's coat and muscles, and let your fingers guide you; let them nurture and experience the connection," Isabella said as she demonstrated with one of the rescue dogs. The diverse group listened closely, and practiced as she demonstrated where to massage, how to be gentle, when to be firm. The dogs stood still and accepted the touch.

The rescue center seemed to take on a new life and became more than a place for rescue, but also a place for healing. Its growing reputation would make it the first of its kind and perhaps a new paradigm for future animal rescue centers. As it grew, Carlos and Isabella became more ambitious.

The center housed a dozen Dogos Argentinos, and only those with a special permit could adopt a Dogo for protection or for purposes related to law enforcement. The Dogo Argentino's reputation as an animal to be feared was known throughout the country. Typically large in stature, white in color, and with short hair that reveals every bulging muscle, Dogos weigh anywhere from forty to sixty kilograms and can often be mistaken for an American pit bull. Dogos are bred for big-game hunting and protection. The Dogo's bite is more powerful than that of a German shepherd, and its movements are faster than a Bengal tiger's. Countless stories tell of Dogos bred to protect their masters only to turn on them and attack with their powerful jaws, tearing the flesh away from the bones—a bloody change of attitude, often leading to the worst outcomes. The Dogos at the center were the biggest challenge of any of the rescued dogs, since many of them had turned on their masters or attacked a family member. Although, oddly enough, some were abandoned for lacking a killer instinct.

The most aggressive and feared Dogo, named Brutus, was so vicious that he was off-limits to everyone. Carlos often fed Brutus through the cage and would communicate with high-pitched tones, hoping to win his trust. He believed there was hope, and one day he let Brutus out into an open area. It was as if a previously caged lion had been let free. Carlos moved cautiously into the space with Brutus, who stood foaming at the mouth. Suddenly, with great speed and force, Brutus lunged, knocked Carlos over, and pinned him to the ground. He stood over him with intense eyes, grit his sharp teeth, and growled, jaw dripping, threatening to take a piece of flesh if Carlos dared try and move. Isabella could hear his vicious intermittent growls and ran to the pen. She spoke softly to Carlos.

"Don't make any sudden moves or he—"

"Are you kidding me? I am stuck; he is just waiting for me to move so he can attack," whispered Carlos. Isabella grabbed a rope and tied a noose; she slowly made her way into the pen area. Brutus turned to her and warned her with a deep threatening growl.

"He wants you to know he is in control. What on earth are we going to do?"

Isabella responded by moving closer to Brutus, who grit his teeth and growled. Isabella slipped the noose around his neck, and he lunged at her while she pulled the noose tight. The pair struggled for control. Carlos regained his composure and grabbed a long metal rod and prodded and poked at Brutus until the two could shut and lock the steel gate behind them.

"Sweetheart, what the hell got into you? Brutus could have ripped either one of us apart in seconds," Isabella admonished Carlos after they both managed to get Brutus back into his secure enclosure.

"It was a foolish idea," admitted Carlos. "I'm lucky you were close by and were able to take control of Brutus before he tore me to shreds. Perhaps we should concentrate on the less aggressive dogs."

"Carlos, for some reason he didn't turn on me. Maybe I should try to work with him; I think he doesn't trust men."

"Are you crazy? I am still shaking with fear after this frightening incident. Brutus is one mean-spirited Dogo. It's far too dangerous. Your theory about men may be right, but if he ever gets his massive jaws into one of your limbs and then shakes you from side to side, I would always feel responsible."

"Well, what can I say? My ambition may be greater than my common sense. Can we try another Dogo? How about Evita? She is not as aggressive," Isabella proposed.

"Frankly Isabella, we're not too sure which ones are vicious, and for all we know, they all are."

"Carlos, I really want to try this and I—"

Carlos interrupted her. "Are you not hearing me? Was this not bad enough? Do you need to have your blood dripping from his mouth? Enough! Is this what I should expect from a woman who has spent her life training or taming animals?"

"Excuse me, but you can be a real bastard sometimes. I have dedicated my life to healing animals," snapped Isabella. "There is a big difference between healing and taming."

"Isabella, these Dogos are not wild horses like your father or grandfather would catch and tame," Carlos said. "They were bred and have natural instincts to attack."

"Well then how could you be so stupid as to enter his caged area? Forget about me thinking to put a muzzle on Brutus—I should put one on you! Don't ever speak about my father or grandfather that way," Isabella screamed.

"What did I say? I am just trying to protect you," Carlos responded in confusion.

"I don't need your protection. I have gotten by just fine for all these years without protection from you or any other men who expressed those same words. You know it's my life, and if I want to tame Brutus or any other Dogo or even you, it's my decision, and I will do as I please. In fact I am not so sure about us anymore," said Isabella with fire in her eyes as she stamped away from Carlos.

CHAPTER SEVENTEEN

Days later, early one Sunday morning, Enzo took his customary drive into town to have coffee with friends and read the newspaper. His friend Pescado was holding up the paper and pointing to a story with a photograph. "Look at this. With all the bad news, finally we have a good story."

"Well, I guess every once in a while we are entitled to some good news. So what is it?" Enzo responded.

"It's a story about these two kids and their dogs. Look at this—it's titled "The Dog Healers." Sweet photo," said Pescado.

"Oh no, let me see that," Enzo said, grabbing for the paper.

"What's with you, Enzo? It's a good story."

After browsing the story for a moment, Enzo looked up at his friends. "I'm not sure if this is a curse or a gift," he said.

"What do you mean by a curse?" asked Pescado.

"I mean, the article doesn't mention my sister, Isabella, but she developed this program at the rescue center. She made a vow never to speak with a reporter again after the Brazilian Derby."

"So what does it say in the story?" another friend asked.

Enzo handed his friend the newspaper. He looked at the headline "The Dog Healers" and a photo of two young volunteers named Veronica and Hector, each massaging a dog. "What is this Kum Nye stuff they are talking about?" his friend asked.

"Oh, just give the paper back to me," said Enzo.

He read to his friends: "'Learning to massage the dogs makes a difference in our lives,' says Hector. 'Kum Nye healing teaches the dogs and families a way to bond forever.'"

"'The dogs love this therapy,' remarks Veronica proudly, all smiles, 'and I feel great as well.'

Since taking on the volunteer experience, the volunteers say they would like to be veterinarians and would devote their lives to caring for dogs."

"It sounds like a wonderful program," Pescado said. "Kids need to have good experiences in their lives. Your sister should be happy about this. It's only a local story; we're not talking about one of the greatest comebacks in the history of horse racing with a woman trainer taking the credit."

"Perhaps you guys are right," Enzo said. "Maybe I am overreacting to this, but I remember the media in Brazil were relentless. Isabella felt suffocated, and man, was she ever infuriated with me for not getting the situation under control. That type of anger I would not wish on any man, even an enemy."

"I know what you mean; she has a wicked temper, especially when she goes off on you."

"Pescado, you have never accepted how she rejected your macho advances," Enzo kidded. "I don't blame her one bit. I mean, what woman finds you appealing? You're not exactly the Don Juan of Mendoza. So, she nearly knocked you out! How many women have slapped that ugly face of yours in the last year? My sister is sweet, and you, my friend—why do you think we call you Pescado? You smell like a fish and you take the bait, man."

The following week, the rescue center was overwhelmed with families wanting to adopt dogs. Nearly a hundred kids signed up to volunteer. This increased volume of interest added a type of stress that the center had not really anticipated.

At their weekly meeting, the contractor brought more worrisome news. "We're on track to have everything ready for the grand opening, with one slight challenge: The building and health inspectors are giving us a difficult time, and we need to get approval and a certificate to occupy and technically operate. ," she told the group. "I'm not getting a warm, fuzzy feeling from them."

"My brother calls them the necessary bastards," Lucy said. "Just about every property project he works on, the necessary bastards come up with something wrong, causing delay after delay."

As if on cue, the building inspector, Guido Mondongo, suddenly appeared with a smile and his trusty clipboard. Short, with a big belly and dark sunglasses, black curly chest hair poked from his shirt collar and he smelled of too much cheap cologne. A chunky gold bracelet knocked against the clipboard as he dramatically made checkmarks while murmuring to himself.

"Good afternoon ladies. I stopped by to make a routine inspection."

"Señor Mondongo, what is it now? We are complying with all the regulations, and you always seem to find something that is wrong," the contractor said.

"How can I expect a group of women to know anything about health and building codes?"

"How dare you speak to us like this! We have met all the codes to the municipalities' satisfaction," Lucy interjected.

"Well I am afraid not, my dear ladies, and it is not a good practice to disrespect the person who is in charge of your approvals. Your collective actions and inactions will only cause you further delays."

"We can't afford to delay the opening," Florencia responded. "Maybe we should . . ."

"Maybe you should what? I did not quite get that. Can I have a few words alone with Señora Isabella?" Mondongo said.

"Sure," Isabella replied with curiosity.

"My dear Isabella, it's better that we speak in private. You seem to be more level-headed than the others," Mondongo said.

"Thanks, but this means a lot to everyone and we can't help but get emotional," Isabella replied.

"Surely you would love to get your approvals, especially with the big event you have planned, and I would like to accommodate you and help you expedite the process, but just as you have things that are important, so do I. Yet your group fails to recognize my power."

"Well, I can help you, but I am not sure what you are looking for," Isabella said.

"Please check with your contractor. She will give you a better idea how this works. Oh, and one more thing. I know you have some upcoming horse races, and I like to make wagers from time to time. Perhaps you can inform me on what the sure bets are and maybe even move the odds in my favor, if you know what I mean?"

"Why you no-good son of a bitch—this is extortion!"

"Extortion? It's simply a small favor I am asking for. In the racing community, it happens all the time and no one seems to get offended. Remember this is an ongoing relationship we are embarking on, and the approval can be given—and God only knows, approvals can be revoked for violations at any time. Have a blessed day, Señora Isabella," Modongo said, bowing his head as he walked away.

Isabella walked back to the women fuming with anger.

"Well what did he say?" the ladies asked.

"He is a no-good bastard. I am so upset, I can't even find words for him and how we will overcome this son of a—" Isabella said as Malbec, feeling her pain and frustration, sidled up beside her to provide her with comfort.

"Let me handle this," interrupted Tamara. "I will talk to my husband; he and the mayor are friends. He should be able to take care of it, unless someone has a special agenda of their own; you never can tell. Let's try to focus on what needs to get done in the meantime."

"In Brazil, your story stimulated a mysterious aura. You were an enigma. This time we can work with the media with planned releases and events. Perhaps we should hire a publicist. This would give us a way to protect your privacy."

"My intuition tells me that our center may become more than just a local story," Isabella said. "I think Carlos can address any concerns the media may have, so let's go with that plan for now. As for me, I want to focus on my work."

"I like the idea of giving certificates to the people who complete the program. It gives the volunteers an accomplishment they can be proud of. Perhaps we should require all people adopting a dog at our center to complete this program," Tamara told Isabella. "We should have more of a professional-type workshop, one that trains veterinarians, dog groomers, or handlers. I think even breeders might like this and incorporate a form of certification to enhance their reputations."

"I agree," Isabella said. "Spiritual healing is natural for dogs; it's the people that need the training."

The grand opening was quickly approaching and, as with most things in life, as the fierce winds gust, there is no easy sailing, only challenges set by the velocity and direction to help navigate in an angry sea. Let out the sails, capture the wind, move your rudder, and embrace the ride. The final challenge was Guido Mondongo. He liked fancy cars, fast women, and the color of green from the central bank. How do men like Señor Mondongo get into a position of power? He is the thorn in your side, the cockroach in the kitchen, but nevertheless, he was the senior building and health official assigned to issuing approvals for the center. He arrived with a clipboard and his list of convoluted violations, justifying reasons to stand in the center's way until he got what he wanted from Isabella.

Isabella and Carlos seemed to enter a challenging time in their relationship. Poor Carlos felt the wrath of her ups and downs and her temper, and he needed to be with his family. Isabella made her life at the center, putting in long hours—often she was the first to arrive and the last to leave. Carlos wondered if this was her way of dealing, or not dealing, with relationships.

She still could not get Brutus out of her mind. Locks and gates clearly separated Brutus from the staff; they were petrified and wouldn't think of daring to get close to his fortress-like cage. Yet Brutus had a mammoth appetite, and this was an assignment that only Carlos would handle. While Carlos was on a trip to Buenos Aires, Isabella was left with the frightening and potentially violent experience of feeding Brutus. She was determined to make a connection with the vicious Dogo, but her subtle attempts resulted in mean-spirited growls, and he would lunge at her like a hungry animal in the wild. Fortunately for Isabella, she felt protected by the steel bars, the only thing that stood between her and Brutus. She was not so concerned with protection; she wanted that connection and was guided by her lifelong passion. Isabella was tenacious, and continued to win him over with his thirst for blood-dripping steak. This was the first step in the process.

Each day, Isabella came closer and waved the meat from side to side; Brutus clearly focused his bulging eyes on the blood-dripping morsels she held. His carnivorous nostrils vibrated back and forth, smelling the intense scent of the beef. As he approached the gate to grab the meat, Isabella looked into his eyes. "Sientate," she commanded with a stern voice while pointing her forefinger at him until he sat. She made him wait and commanded him to sit before he could indulge. With each small sign of progress they made, Isabella rewarded Brutus with a taste of the blood-oozing steak and in high-pitched tones she praised him. "Bueno mucha-cho, Brutus. Good boy, mi amore."

Each day, they made small strides of progress. The vicious growls relaxed until finally they subsided. Brutus was responding to her commands, and was rewarded with blood-dripping meats. He seemed to appreciate their interaction, the varied sweet sounds of her voice. Brutus tilted his head and looked into her eyes as if he understood that she was a person he could learn to trust. Before long, Isabella was able to have Brutus act on her command and sit attentively, and she even massaged him around his ears through the gate. From all signs, Brutus was intelligent, yet Isabella knew he had the potential to be cunning and turn on her. Still, if her gut feeling was correct, they might just melt the ice together.

The next week, Isabella thought she and Brutus were ready for a personal engagement. She opened the steel gate just at the moment poor Hector was passing by. Without warning, Brutus lunged at Hector and pinned him to the ground. Brutus stood over him and grit his teeth. Before he got ornery, Isabella grabbed him by the collar and with a very firm tone told him, "No!" Brutus froze; he actually responded to her command.

"Sientate," Isabella commanded. Brutus sat still with a guilty look on his face, waiting for her next command. Hector turned white with fear; so nervous, his crotch area darkened with urine. He dared not make a move. Without hesitating, Isabella put her hands on Brutus and began to massage his head and ears. The tension left Brutus's body, and as Isabella moved her hands down his back she could feel his muscles relax.

Isabella gasped with disbelief, amazed that she had made a connection with Brutus without a violent incident. "Hector, look. Look! I knew it, I just knew he would come around," she whispered.

Hector was still frozen to the ground, so Isabella spoke softly to him. "Hector, be careful not to startle him. Slide your body away from us very slowly and keep your distance."

"Trust me, Isabella, I wouldn't think of getting within ten meters of that dog, even if he were behind the bars," replied Hector. "I'm happy for you, but I think you should put a muzzle on him and put him back in his cell. That is one mean Dogo."

"Please, Hector, not a word of this to anyone," Isabella said. "Don't tell the press, and please don't tell Carlos. Promise me you won't tell a soul. Carlos would kill me if he knew about this and I would never hear the end of it."

"I promise. I won't say a word."

"Hector, what you've just witnessed is a huge breakthrough in Brutus's behavior. I'm convinced that his previous owner was nasty and beat him. I'll bet Brutus took a bite out of him and I'm sure he deserved it. This must be the reason Brutus is so aggressive toward men. But look—he's intelligent; he listened, and notice how he calmed from being massaged."

Each day Isabella secretly worked with Brutus; no one would ever think he was the same animal. Who would believe that a once-vicious beast had become a happy pooch? Isabella was so excited that she lost track of time, and before she knew it, Carlos returned. He greeted her with a big hug, yet Isabella was not so endearing. Perhaps, still angered by the demeaning remark he made about her father and grandfather.

"Hola, my darling. How was your week?" he asked.

With a touch of guilt, she replied, "The usual. Maestro managed to unlock the gates and his loyal pack busted out, and while they were out Linguini stole their food, but otherwise things have been uneventful—no dog fights, no injuries."

"I leave you in charge for one week and that's all you have to say? It's like your mind is someplace else. Are you hiding something from me?" he asked in a suspicious tone.

"I am sorry. You're right; I have other things on my mind."

"Well, are you okay?" Carlos asked, concerned.

"Yes, ta bien. We've been completely inundated with people signing up to volunteer, as well as families and older folks who want to adopt and attend the workshop. Even some vets and dog handlers from Buenos Aires want to learn more about our program."

Carlos blinked with amazement. "For the love of the dogs, I can't figure out how such a diverse cross section of people heard about our program. They're already waiting in line and we've not even formally started." Carlos laughed. "My dear Isabella, it just goes to show us that people love their dogs. No domestic fights, no separations, and no divorces; we bond for life and that's just the way it is."

"Yes, what was I thinking? But I am not too sure about us." She laughed gently. "Carlos, with so much going on we need a full-time director. This place is getting really crazy and one of us should take charge. Personally, I think it should be you. What do you think?"

"I think you're right about a full-time director of operations," Carlos responded. "But shouldn't it be you? What about my responsibility to my mother and sisters? I also have my commitments with Florencia, Roberto, and Moisés."

"In due time we'll figure it out," Isabella assured him.

"No, we need a plan now! Soon you will be back at the ranch working with Tango and I'll be faced with these dilemmas. And there's no question that I must fulfill the commitment I have with Roberto and Moisés."

"Carlos, I understand your concerns, but we need you at the helm here. Let me talk to Florencia. She's a woman who knows how to get things done and she may have a good solution."

"No, Isabella, this is between you and me. Are we working together on this, or will you always put me off with your friends? Where do I stand with you?"

"Carlos! Why do you say it like that? You're very important to me, but we have a lot of work to do. You are either a part of this, and as dedicated as the rest of us, or you're letting your emotions get the best of you. I'm not going on vacation, I'm going to *work*."

And thus it was official—Carlos had become the acting director of the Mendoza Dog Rescue Center. For the next ten days, he and Isabella worked together organizing the adoption and training programs. They also focused on development of a program that would teach dogs to provide assistance and therapy for sick, injured, and disabled people.

The contractors finished work on the building, and Tamara's husband had somehow persuaded the mayor's office to intercede on their behalf. The certificate of occupancy was expected to arrive any day.

Isabella and Carlos planned to celebrate that weekend, believing that their approvals would come through. When Officer Mondongo arrived again with a smile, they thought that he came with good news.

"Hola, Señora Isabella and Carlos. As always, it's good to see you," Mondongo said.

"Officer Mondongo, it's good to see you. I guess you have some good news for us?"

"Well yes, I have some good news and some not-so-good news. The good news is, I spoke with the mayor and he informed me that one of your associates paid him a visit. The bad news is that the mayor is just a political puppet controlled by my people, and he unfortunately has no control over building codes and approvals. So please, let me be clear. This place will never be allowed to open without my approvals, and if you plan to move forward without meeting the municipality's building and health codes, I will have to shut you down—even if I have to do this the day of your event," he said.

"But we thought everything was taken care of," Carlos and Isabella chimed in unison.

"Well, you thought wrong again. Do I make myself clear? Have a wonderful weekend," Mondongo said.

"Oh my God, what are we going to do?" said Carlos.

"This guy is the biggest loser. I should have my brothers pay him a visit and rough him up. God help us. We need something, and more than a prayer," Isabella said as Carlos embraced her.

CHAPTER EIGHTEEN

From time to time, Enzo stopped by the center to see how things were coming along. On this day, he arrived with some big news and spoke to Isabella and Carlos in the office.

"Isabella, I know you're busy with final preparations, but I just heard from Ricardo. He entered Tango in Clásico El Ensayo, the most important horse race in Chile. This race rivals the Brazilian Derby! It's held at Club Hípico de Santiago, Chile's oldest race-track. It's the most prestigious horse race in all of South America. Tango is on his way to the ranch and should arrive sometime to-morrow. We need you to come home and prepare Tango for the race. The champion needs his special trainer."

"I will be there for my champion," Isabella confirmed excitedly.

"What about the center's opening?" Carlos asked.

"You are the director; you can handle things until my return. I will be back for opening day," Isabella replied. Carlos rolled his eyes and walked off. Isabella waved her hands dismissively as Enzo stared at the ground.

Isabella arrived at the ranch the following day. As she approached the field she saw that Enzo was riding Tango. When she called out to Enzo, Tango heard her voice and galloped with great speed to greet her, nearly shaking Enzo from the saddle. Within seconds, Isabella and Tango were reunited, and Isabella hugged Tango as he nudged his head into her body.

She closed her eyes and let her fingers feel his energy and release any tension in his muscles. She looked at Enzo. "What do you think of his condition?" she asked.

"He's in pretty good shape, but we need him at his best for El Ensayo."

"Of course, but Tango and I need some time alone. I'll take him for a short ride and bring him back to the stall soon."

"He's all yours for the next few weeks," Enzo said with a smile.

Isabella and Tango wandered into the wilderness. She paid close attention to his movement and pace as he galloped proudly through the field and up the trail. When they reached Echo's Peak, the place close to their hearts, they looked across a stunning valley laced with brooks flowing from the Andes, a smattering of pine trees, and blooming flowers in the fields. The winds whistled and blew the strong medicinal fragrance of the pines; hawks circled the landscape and clouds floated through the clear blue sky. This was a place to feel free.

Isabella and Tango were at peace as they remained still, absorbing the pink-hewed sunset in the valley of paradise. On their way back to the ranch, Isabella pondered the upcoming Clásico El Ensayo. She anticipated a field with cunning jockeys notorious for sabotaging the favorites. The days of running a good, clean, honest race were long gone, and Tango would be the horse to target.

"So, Isabella, how was your ride?" Enzo asked.

"It was wonderful; we connected with every living species in the wilderness," Isabella replied with a warm smile as she wrapped her arms around Tango's muscular neck. "He's in good shape," Isabella told Enzo, "but he's got a long way to go."

"Will he be ready in time for the race?"

"I think so."

"Remember what I said to you about the other jockeys; they're all out to get him. Word on the track is that they're going to squeeze him or take him down."

"Yes, I know. Tango will be fine; but I have my reservations about Mario, his trainer. I can't place my finger on it. Luca was also a bit distant at our last meeting."

"Perhaps you are being a bit paranoid, but then again, I have learned to never underestimate your intuitions," Enzo noted with a puzzled look.

The next morning, Isabella caught up with her brothers. They sat around the table gulping dark, aromatic coffee and gorging on fresh-baked croissants. They glanced in her direction, impatient, with nervous anticipation for some feedback.

Francisco finally spoke. "So what do you think? It's going to be a tough race; these guys are still in denial over the Brazilian Derby. They want everyone to think it was a fluke and they'll do whatever they can to keep a female trainer out of the limelight."

Isabella responded with her usual confidence. "They can have all the limelight they want. At the end of the race, there can be only one champion, and if I have my way, the champion will be Tango. But I can't sit around the breakfast table talking about this or wringing my hands with worry. Tango and I have work to do."

Down at the barn, Isabella reached up to Tango and moved her fingertips from his head to his tail and back. This was Tango's checkup. She worked with Tango every day. Their routine alternated between riding, therapeutic massage, and aquatic therapy in the hot springs. Isabella could feel how their long rides each morning taxed Tango's body, but still it was necessary training for endurance and his stamina. Her gift for massage would always bring them together. She would close her eyes and allow her fingers feel her way and guide her to the muscles that needed the most attention.

She liked to start around his head and whisper sweet sounds for his pleasure. Her strong hands and fingers worked her way around his backside and then into his upper thighs. She pushed and rotated her palms, pressing with a circular motion into his muscles. Isabella and Tango were at peace as she ended the session by scratching him from head to hoof. To complete the day, they both soaked in the soothing hot waters of the mineral spring.

Every evening just before sunset, she and Tango rode to Echo's Peak. It was as if Mother Nature herself beckoned them to this place. As they looked out into the picturesque valley, Isabella placed her arms around Tango and whispered softly in his ear, "Look at the beauty that surrounds us; breathe deep and inhale the scents of nature; listen for the creatures in the wild and absorb their collective energy, and feel the freedom of the clouds blowing in the wind." Tango moved his head up and down as if he understood.

Isabella had been so focused on Tango that she had forgotten about the outside world, so for the sake of keeping the peace, she called Carlos. "Mi amor," she said sweetly, "I apologize for not keeping in touch. Other than my work with Tango, I've lost sight of everything. Please forgive me. How is it going?"

"Wow, you can be like a faucet, warm one day and cold the next. I have been trying to reach you and you are never available. For a woman that connects so well with animals, you leave me wondering at times. Perhaps in my next life I should reincarnate as a dog or a horse? Everybody's working hard getting ready for the big opening ceremony. Tamara has invited her friends from Buenos Aires, Veronica and Hector have invited many locals from Mendoza, and Florencia has invited some wealthy people from all over to fly in for the event."

"Wow, it sounds crazy, but good," Isabella said, impressed.

"Yes, very crazy. Maestro opened Brutus's gate, which caused a major chain of events. Otherwise, I've been focused on taking care of the dogs and processing applicants, but there simply isn't enough time in the day with everything going on. Everyone seems to want a dog now, and we just don't have the manpower."

"Carlos, whatever you do, please don't stress out over this. Remember the words of Jamyang: 'Stress is a killer.'"

"I know, Isabella, and I'm trying my best, but you make me crazy. It would be nice to know where we stand. About the ceremony—do you think it's a good idea? The media is going to be all over this and I am not sure it will be any different than it was in Brazil. Except that perhaps you will lash out at me instead of Enzo," Carlos said.

"Carlos, I was overwhelmed, and Enzo was hungover. How would you expect me to react?" Isabella replied.

"I am a bit overwhelmed myself; I wish you were with me," Carlos said.

"You'll do fine, Carlos. Just follow your heart and trust your instincts. I promise, after the next race I will do my best to work on our relationship. Please just bear with me."

The week before El Ensayo, Ricardo had made arrangements for Luca and Mario to work with Tango under Isabella's direction to provide vigorous daily workouts, followed by Kum Nye massage and therapeutic baths in the soothing mineral spring. Afterward, she would stretch Tango out and whisper to him. For their final preparation, Isabella's brothers gathered their most ornery stallions to simulate a race to prepare Tango for any potential onslaught from the fierce competitors in Chile.

CHAPTER NINETEEN

The day after the race simulation, Ricardo and Lucy arrived in Mendoza. Enzo met them at the airport and drove them to the ranch. "Please let me take your bags. I am sure Isabella is somewhere close."

Ricardo followed the sound of boisterous laughter and chatting behind the ranch house. He was stunned at the sight of bottles of wine spread around the table—it was an afternoon party.

"What the hell is this? Is this what I pay you for? I thought we might be training for the race," shouted Ricardo.

"Ricardo, I know how this looks, but we've been working hard, and our afternoon family gatherings are important to us. We need this time to unwind a bit, and I think it is about time you just join us and unwind yourself. Trust me, this is essential. Tango is as good as he can be; the other jockeys will taste the dirt from the thunder of his hooves. The trophy will be ours."

Isabella's words and confidence helped calm Ricardo's nerves. Enzo and Francisco passed out ornate wine goblets used for special occasions and poured a generous serving of their translucent maroon-colored Malbec for the guests. Enzo took a silver spoon and tapped on his glass before speaking.

"There can be only one champion at Club Hípico. Please, everyone, a toast to our next trophy—at El Ensayo." With great gusto, everyone raised glasses and sipped the fruits of the family vineyard.

After the grand toast, it was time to move on to Santiago, Chile. Enzo pulled the truck and trailer up to the barn and Isabella escorted Tango inside.

"Please, fly to Santiago with us," Ricardo said to Isabella. "The flight is just forty minutes."

"Thanks all the same," Isabella said, "but I must stay with Tango. You never can tell what might happen as you pass through the Andes."

"Are you sure?" asked Ricardo. "It's a long ride through the mountains."

"I'm positive, Ricardo. Trust me. I need to do this."

"If you insist," Ricardo said. "But if we win the race, you must fly back with us. And I won't take no for an answer."

"That's okay with me, but listen, Ricardo, I absolutely must be with Tango for the ride through the mountains. The weather can be unpredictable and treacherous."

Isabella and Enzo began their journey, driving through the grand ranches and sprawling vineyards and olive farms until they reached the charming foothills. Before long, they started the climb through the great Andes mountains. After several hours, Isabella insisted they stop and let Tango out for a good stretch and some fresh mountain air. They were about two thousand meters above sea level and the temperature was dropping quickly, so Isabella took Tango's favorite alpaca blanket and placed it over his body. She reached into her studded leather bag and mixed some therapeutic herbs from her garden that would help Tango relax and breathe easier in higher altitudes.

Isabella joined Enzo in the truck and they climbed higher. The air became thinner, the temperature continued dropping, and the winding road narrowed. They moved slowly as they passed a sign that placed them at 3,490 meters above sea level.

"Look, the Chilean border is only five kilometers from here," Enzo told Isabella.

Isabella sighed with relief. "Good news. This cold mountain altitude is not so good for Tango. Once we pass through the border, we'll begin our descent, and that will be a blessing for us all."

As she rummaged through her bag looking for a snack, Enzo came to a complete stop. Before them was a line of nearly a hundred trucks. For some ungodly reason, they were at a standstill, lined up—not a typical scenario for this particular border crossing.

"What the hell is going on? This never happens!" exclaimed Enzo.

Isabella looked up, and with good reason to be alarmed, asked, "What is it? Something must be seriously wrong."

Enzo threw his hands up and looked out the window. "I don't believe this, and it couldn't happen at a worse time."

"We have to pull over!" Isabella was panicky.

"Isabella, if we stop here, who knows if these bastards will let us back in line? We can't risk it."

"God damn it, Enzo, I can't take it anymore! I need to be with Tango, and I am not going to leave him alone."

"You will freeze in the trailer! I checked the heaters before we left and one of them is out. We're almost four thousand meters above sea level, the sun is setting soon, and you will freeze!"

"*I* will freeze? What about *Tango*? I can't believe you allowed him to travel through the mountains with only one heater. Well, you'd better think of something quickly."

"Just a minute," Enzo said, and picked up the transmitter of his citizens band radio. "Hola, hola! Please, anybody! This is Señor Borello. I have an emergency situation. What's the problem here?"

A voice crackled back over the speakers in the dashboard. "The border patrol is short on staff. I think they're in the midst of a strike."

"The God damn strikes can even reach the peaks of the Andes! You must be joking—what can they be striking over? Only in Argentina . . ."

"Wait a minute. Enzo, is that you?" a voice inquired.

"Si," Enzo answered, grinning as he recognized the voice on the CB. "Lorenzo! How are you doing?"

"Not bad," Lorenzo said. "Hell of a game last weekend, huh?"

"Yeah, great game, but leave your ringer behind next game. You pissed off my teammates and you know it's against the rules."

"What?" Lorenzo exclaimed with false indignation. "It's bocce, my friend, and no rules forbid it. Anyway, what are you doing here? This is no place for a gaucho boy like you, and I don't wish this trip on anyone."

"Lorenzo, my sister and I are transporting a racehorse to El Ensayo in Santiago. We have a serious crisis. One of the heaters in the trailer is out. Unfortunately, I never anticipated this and I am not sure how long the horse can withstand the freezing conditions."

"What's the horse's name?" asked Lorenzo.

"Tango."

"Get the hell out of here. You mean *the* Tango? The Brazilian Derby champion?"

"Yes, *the* Tango. Anyway, can you tell me how long will it take until we can pass through the border?"

"We could be here for three, maybe four hours," Lorenzo told him.

Enzo groaned. "My crazy sister left the cab; she's with Tango in the trailer. Tango's muscles will tighten like a pulled bow, and this is a catastrophic situation. If they're lucky enough to make it through this, Tango will be in no condition to run the race."

"All right, hold on," said Lorenzo. "Let me make a call to my sister."

"I don't understand how your sister can help."

Lorenzo laughed. "Are you kidding me? The woman turns heads, she stops traffic—we are talking about the most sensuous flower in the valley of Mendoza. I thought you knew her, man. Once you meet her you will understand."

"What on earth are you talking about? We are almost four thousand meters high in the middle of the Andes freezing our co-jónes off, the border guards are striking, and Tango may be forced to forfeit. I wouldn't be surprised if someone paid off the border patrol to keep him from running."

"You're being paranoid, but about my sister—she sleeps with the captain of the border patrol. Need I say more? Please, I will call her immediately and get back to you shortly."

———

Lorenzo picked up his mobile phone and called his sister Evita.

"Hola."

"Evita, it's Lorenzo. I am transporting a load of fruit through the Andes. We are at a standstill at the border and our buns are as cold as ice. Listen, there is a major crisis here and I need a big favor, one that only you can provide."

"Anything for you—what's wrong?"

"My friend Enzo and his sister are transporting a horse named Tango to Chile for El Ensayo, and they fear the scorn of the Andes will take a horrendous toll on him, that he may even have to forfeit the race. The heater in their trailer is out, and who knows, he and Isabella may freeze to death."

"Oh my God! You're talking about *the* Tango, the horse that made the greatest comeback in the history of horse racing?"

"Yes, *the* Tango."

"All right, I'll call Bruno right away and see what he can do. He will want a present for this favor. You know the way things work."

"Sister, give him whatever he wants. This is urgent."

"Okay," Evita said. "Give me a few minutes." Evita hung up and quickly dialed.

"Hola, Bruno. It's me, Evita, your sweet fragrant flower."

"Hola, my darling, how are you today? It's very quiet and lonely up here. Perhaps you can come and join me; we can melt the ice together," Bruno said.

"I would love to, Bruno, but at the moment I need a special favor."

"You know it will cost you . . . but what is it, my flower?"

Evita explained the crisis, and moments after they said good-bye, Captain Bruno took control.

Lorenzo clutched his phone, nervously waiting to hear from Evita. His phone finally rang. "Hola, Lorenzo. I just got off the phone with my Captain Bruno, and he said not to worry, he will take care of this crisis, but he wants a small favor. A suite at El Ensayo and dinner at the clubhouse with the best champagne money can buy."

"Whatever he wants. I will do my best to make it happen." Lorenzo picked up his CB microphone and radioed for Enzo.

"What's going on?" he asked.

"My sister spoke to Captain Bruno; he's willing to help, but it will cost you."

"Of course it is going to cost—the question is, how much?"

"He wants a suite for El Ensayo, dinner at the clubhouse, and the finest champagne available."

"No problem," Enzo said. "You have my word, but how on earth is he going to take care of this? We must be five kilometers from the border and we're moving slower than a turtle."

"Maybe he can bring a portable heater," Lorenzo said. "At least that will help keep Isabella and Tango warm. Anyway, I need to talk to my sister again, but before I do I have one more small favor to ask, Enzo."

"What's that?"

"I would really like to take my wife and two kids to the race," said Lorenzo. "Can you arrange for another suite?"

"I'll see what I can do," Enzo told him.

"Thank you, mi amigo."

Enzo coaxed Isabella back into the heated cabin of the truck, despite her protests, and filled her in on his conversation with Lorenzo. He prayed that Evita was as alluring and persuasive as Lorenzo had implied.

CHAPTER TWENTY

Within minutes, an envoy of Argentine and Chilean border patrol soldiers arrived; it was like the parting of the Red Sea. They closed off an entire lane and proceeded down the road in three military jeeps, searching for Enzo. Captain Bruno's voice blasted through a loudspeaker.

"Enzo Borello, this is Captain Bruno of the Argentine border patrol. Please flash your lights so we can identify you. All other vehicles are instructed to turn your lights off."

One by one, the truckers' lights went off, and the mountain road went dark. As the soldiers approached Enzo's vehicle, he heard the announcement and frantically flashed his lights on and off. The three jeeps pulled up to Enzo's truck and a big, burly, uniformed man stepped out of one of the vehicles and walked over to him.

"Are you Enzo Borello?"

"Yes, sir. I am Enzo Borello."

"I'm Captain Bruno, commander of the border patrol. I am sorry I could not find a portable heater, but here is a blanket." He passed a handwoven blanket into the cabin to Isabella and she draped it over herself.

"Captain, we have a champion racehorse in the trailer and we are desperate for help to avoid a catastrophic wait in this frigid temperature," Enzo said. "At this rate, we could be stuck here for hours."

Captain Bruno nodded. "Young man, I couldn't agree more." He signaled to his second-in-command, then turned back to Enzo. "As commander of the Argentine border patrol, I order you to follow me; I believe Tango has a race to run."

The second-in-command signaled with his high-powered flashlight for Enzo to move his truck and horse trailer into the lane they had cleared and follow the border guards' jeeps. Within minutes, they arrived at the border checkpoint and were instructed to come directly to Captain Bruno's office. God had answered Enzo's prayer.

Captain Bruno leaned over and kissed Isabella on the cheek. Isabella threw her arms around Captain Bruno in gratitude. "You're a lifesaver, and I don't know how we can ever repay you."

He took out his official stamp, saying, "It's quite all right. Passports, por favor?"

As she presented their passports, Isabella leaned over and kissed Bruno on the cheek.

"Make us proud," he said, stamping their passports. "I'll see you in the winner's circle."

"Thank you," Isabella said. "God willing, we will *all* be in the winner's circle."

"I know you must be on your way, but please have some hearty homemade soup first," Bruno offered.

Enzo and Isabella were exhausted and famished.

"Ah, it's delicious. Thank you so much, mi Capitan," Isabella said with a smile.

They climbed back into their vehicle and the Chilean border patrol escorted them into Chile, down the mountainside, and through a treacherous area until it was safe. As they passed the line of truckers stalled on the Chilean side, the truckers flashed their lights and sounded their horns. Enzo and Isabella felt an instant relief, enough to laugh about this unusual experience.

The second-in-command pulled his jeep alongside the truck and motioned for Enzo to open his window.

"We will be cheering for Tango. Good luck in the race."

"Muchas gracias, we are so grateful for your help," Enzo told him.

Isabella called out to the patrolman, "Please, I forgot to return this blanket. Would you see that Captain Bruno gets it?"

Shortly after they parted ways with the border patrol, Enzo and Isabella pulled into a rest stop to check on Tango. She was afraid that he had been traumatized, and pulled him quickly from the trailer, vigorously rubbing every inch of his body to warm him up. His body was shivering and his hind muscles went into spasms. The mountain ride with one heater was more than he could handle. Isabella broke a heavy sweat from nurturing him back to warmth until she was satisfied with his condition.

"How is Tango?

"We are most fortunate for everyone's help at the border. He stopped shivering and his body feels like it's warmed up. My Tango is resilient, but please, can we be on our way to Santiago?"

Later that evening, Isabella called Carlos.

"Hey, sweetie, how are you doing?" she asked.

"I'm a little stressed, but okay," he admitted. "How was the ride to Santiago?"

"It was certainly a ride I'll never forget, but we're here at last and making final preparations for tomorrow's race. How are things going in Mendoza?"

"We've just about finished preparations for tomorrow's grand opening. Tonight we are entertaining some people. Everyone is excited about tomorrow's race and we hope to celebrate Tango's big victory."

"From Brazil to Chile," sighed Isabella.

"Are you going to be back in time for the ceremony?" asked Carlos.

"I wouldn't miss it for the world. It will be a weekend to remember."

"That's for sure. Before we hang up, Tamara wants to talk to you."

"Hello, Isabella?" Tamara was giddy with wine.

"Hi, Tamara! Good to hear your voice."

"We miss you."

"I wish I could be there with the canine team—but soon enough. We just need to get through this race," Isabella said.

"We are with you in spirit, my dear. No matter what happens, we love you. But before we say goodbye, I want you to know we have something special for your return."

"Honestly? Tell me."

Tamara laughed. "My dear, it will be more special if we leave it as a nice surprise."

CHAPTER TWENTY-ONE

The morning of the race, Enzo and Isabella met Lucy and Ricardo for breakfast in a little café.

"How was the ride from Mendoza?" asked Ricardo as he sipped his cappuccino.

Isabella and Enzo looked at each other and knew it was best not to make him any more nervous than he was. "The ride was certainly an adventure," Enzo told him. "And memorable at that."

"Ah, good," Lucy said. "Life's adventures are moments of memories."

"Definitely," Isabella agreed.

"How's Tango feeling?" asked Ricardo.

"Tango is doing fine," she said. "The ride was a little tough on him. Next time, we should leave earlier and plan on spending more time at the race site."

Ricardo gave Isabella a nervous stare for a few seconds.

As usual, Enzo noticed his unease and tried to reassure him. "We will make you proud today, rest assured."

Ricardo took a deep breath and nodded. "I will be proud when I see him first across the finish line."

"On that note," Isabella said, finishing her croissant, "I should head to the track and help them get ready." She stood up and took her leave.

Isabella spent the next hours working with Tango, and she made their last moments before the race quiet and intimate. She held his head close and whispered in his ears.

"Just imagine that we are at Echo's Peak with all the wonders of nature. Feel the crisp fresh air, smell the sweet fragrance from the pines, listen to the hawks cry as they glide with grace through the sky," she said with a soft tone. "Today you will run for the kingdom of the wilderness and show them the powerful spirit of the free and wild." Tango nudged his head against her and stomped his hooves into the dirt.

An hour before the race, Tango's jockey, Luca, dressed in a brilliant navy blue outfit, showed up.

"Hola, Miss Isabella," Luca said

"Hola, Luca. What is it? You look a bit pale." Isabella said with a concerned look.

"I was fine this morning, but sometime after breakfast with Mario, I began to feel a bit queasy. Perhaps it's nerves, or the water. Mario insisted I hydrate myself for the change in altitude," Luca replied.

"Speaking of Mario, where is he? I mean, he is the official trainer and he should be here with you and Tango," Isabella said worriedly.

"We were together just ten minutes ago and he excused himself when two dark-skinned, well-dressed men came over to talk with him in private. I know he mentioned that he was going to the box office to place a bet on the race," Luca said.

"Speaking of bets, I need to take care of mine. Remember, keep a tight rein, and whatever you do, don't let the other jockeys box you into the center of the field," she emphasized to Luca. "I am going to find Mario; he needs to be with you."

Isabella entered the stadium. She could not believe how magnificent a setting it was. The Club Hípico is like no other racetrack in the world. It is 520 meters above sea level, nestled in the valley of Santiago, Chile, surrounded by the ice-capped Andes mountains. The air is fresh and clean and the temperature is cooler than most tracks, creating an optimal environment for the racehorses. On her way to the betting booth, she noticed Mario and the two well-dressed men, one of whom slipped him a bulging white envelope. Taken by the scene, she moved closer and hid behind a pillar to listen in on the conversation.

"You can count on me," Mario said. "Luca will be lucky if he finishes the race. Now if you will excuse me, with your generosity, I need to make my bet and get back to Tango and Luca."

Isabella panicked. She watched Mario place substantial bets on the two favorites, boxing them to win and place second. Oh my God, I knew he was no good—what a sinister scoundrel, she thought to herself. She looked at the time and hurried to Ricardo's suite.

When Isabella arrived at Ricardo's suite, she was surprised to find Evita and Captain Bruno sitting next to Ricardo and Lucy. More alarming, however, was a gentleman wearing a Chilean military uniform; it was the captain of the Chilean border patrol and his wife. The two officers must have had a couple of drinks. They were boasting and laughing about how they had helped Enzo and Isabella, saying that if it had not been for their doing, Tango could still be stuck trying to cross the border.

Lucy looked at Isabella. "What happened?"

"Let's just say it was quite an adventure, and we should all be very grateful to these two captains for making sure we made it here on time," Isabella said, a modest, diplomatic smile playing at the corners of her mouth.

CHAPTER TWENTY-TWO

The thirty-minute horn sounded as the odds came on the board. To their surprise, Tango was not listed as the favorite, and his odds were just 8–1. Two other horses were favored over Tango.

"What the hell is going on?" Ricardo said, his eyes ablaze. "Eight to one? We should be the favorite, especially after his performance in the Brazilian Derby!"

Enzo, for all his frustration, let loose a sigh of resignation. "Would you like a drink, Ricardo?"

"Might as well," he replied grumpily.

Isabella had no time to worry about the odds; she had pressing priorities, and flew out of her seat and hurried back to Tango's stall. Luca was white as a ghost and hunched over a bucket, vomiting, as if he had been poisoned. Mario stood just next to him wearing a sinister smile.

Isabella ran up from behind, pushed Mario to the ground, and punched him in the face. "You no-good bastard, you put something in his food or water—you poisoned him!"

"What are you talking about, have you lost your mind? The poor guy is sick!" Mario replied.

"I saw you take the money from those two guys and place a bet on their horses. That's what I am talking about!"

Luca heaved again into the bucket. "What do you mean? Is it true?" he asked in a weak, sickly tone.

"Just get out of my sight," Isabella screamed. "It *is* true," she said to Luca, holding his head.

The two-minute horn sounded as the trainers escorted their horses onto the track. The jockeys brightened the field as in a fashion show, their silks in shades of ruby red, emerald green, royal purple, magenta, lemon yellow, and deep turquoise. The scene for the fans was breathtaking.

"Where is Tango?" Ricardo screamed.

"Where is Isabella?" Enzo cried nervously as he looked for her.

Just then, Tango entered the track, barely in time for the start.

"Holy mother, it looks like Isabella is riding Tango! What on earth is going on?" Lucy said with a puzzled look.

"That's what I would like to know," Ricardo said.

"What about Mario and Luca?" Enzo said.

The high-spirited horses pranced to the gate, and the cool mountain air energized the stadium. Raucous fans cheered, and the echoes of their enthusiasm could be heard across the distant mountains. As the field of stallions entered the starting gate, the crowd quieted, awaiting the sound of the horns and the synchronized starting guns.

"This is going to be one fantastic race," Captain Bruno declared, after he had a few stiff drinks.

"Something doesn't feel right. Why is Isabella riding Tango? Where are your jockey and trainer?" Enzo asked Ricardo.

"There is something very wrong with this picture," Ricardo answered in a cold sweat.

"Have faith in Isabella. If anyone can ride Tango to victory, it's she," Lucy said.

The announcer boomed with the news. "What's this? It looks like a woman is riding Tango. This is certainly a first in the history of El Ensayo."

At the gate, Isabella leaned over Tango and gave him her final whispers. The horns sounded, the synchronized starting guns fired, and the horses blasted out of the gates, their pounding hooves trampling the wide right-handed turf course. Spectators could see each exhalation the horses made as their breath came in contact with the cool air of the Andes. Throughout the stadium, fans cheered for their favorites.

It was a pretty even field for the first quarter of the race. As they approached the halfway mark, the two favorites, Vientos de Fuego and Galápagos, were running in third and fourth position, and just as Isabella had anticipated, Tango was now boxed in by them—she had to back off and find another way through the pack.

Gradually the field spread but Tango was still in trouble; the Chileans were notorious for squeezing the horse they decided to target. Ricardo and Enzo watched in horror as the horses headed into the final turn. This could not be happening. Tango was stuck with no way to break out.

Lucy chanted at the top of her lungs, "Free and wild! Free and wild!" Suddenly, Tango burst through the field, making his way gradually into the fourth position while the two favorites led the pack, neck and neck. They came into the homestretch, but Tango was still a good length behind. As he advanced into third and began to close in fast on the leaders, Enzo and Lucy shouted, "Tango, free and wild!"

The captains and their ladies took up the cry and the mantra spread throughout the stands.

"TANGO, FREE AND WILD! TANGO, FREE AND WILD!"

As the crowd chanted, the three horses thundered toward the finish line, neck and neck. They shot across the finish line but, alarmingly, there was no clear winner. Arguments broke out throughout the stands over which horse had won the race. Five minutes passed and there was still no word from the judges, who were examining the video footage and camera angles. All the while, the fans continued to bicker, proclaiming their horse as the winner.

Finally, at an impasse themselves, the judges invited all three horses and their riders to come onto the field so that the crowd could decide the winner. This was unprecedented at Club Hípico.

The senior judge—a respected figure in the racing world—walked over to the winner's circle and took the microphone. "As you all know, Club Hípico is the oldest and most prestigious track in all of South America. Since 1870 we have never had as close and as exciting a race as the one we witnessed today. We have decided to show you the footage of the finish and let it be your call."

He gestured to a large screen, and it flickered on to show the spectators the final 15 meters of the race from an inside angle. The crowd turned its attention to the multiple TV monitors for all to view the disputed finish. The greatly favored horse from Ecuador, named Galápagos, had thrust his body into the lead and, from his midsection down, appeared to be the winner. The crowd cheered for the favorite, but as they examined the finish from another angle they, saw Tango push his neck and head forward over the finish line; it appeared that he had won by a nose. Still there were murmurs of indecision from the crowd, punctuated by the sounds of more quarreling.

From the left side, the second judge tapped on the chief judge's shoulder and spoke quietly into his ear. Then the third of the judges' panel joined them from the right. The three argued among themselves and finally, the well-dressed judge in the middle tapped on the microphone, nodded, and addressed the crowd once more.

"Ladies and gentlemen, as you can see, this was an incredibly close race, and as such, it was most difficult for us to determine the winner. However, it has been brought to my attention that there was one more angle that we should have examined—the one you just viewed on the monitors. With that in mind, it has been decided unanimously by the judges that the winner of the 2010 Clásico El Ensayo is Tango from Brazil."

The crowd went crazy. Screams of "TANGO, FREE AND WILD!" echoed throughout the stadium. Ricardo, Lucy, Enzo, and guests were stomping the bleachers and hugging one another; as they cast their eyes on Isabella, tears were streaming down her cheeks.

Ricardo and Lucy made their way to the winner's circle. Ricardo looked at Isabella with puzzled eyes and addressed the noisy fans as camera flashes lit the stadium.

"Today's race is one for the record books of El Ensayo," Ricardo began. "We watched the noblest horses and jockeys compete, but as you know, this exciting finish can only bring one champion to the winner's circle. Today that great champion is Tango.

"I would like to thank my team for their hard work and dedication, and I would also like to extend my thanks to Captains Bruno and Fuego of the Argentinean and Chilean border patrols, respectively, and to Captain Bruno's partner Evita, a woman of great talent and great persuasion." Scattered laughter erupted throughout the crowd. "She made things happen for Tango and helped his team get through the difficult terrain at the border in the Andes. If it were not for her, this victory would not have been possible."

The crowd offered Ricardo, Tango, and Isabella a standing ovation. Tango's neck was wreathed in a blanket of vibrant yellow roses, and he held his head proudly, as only a champion can. It was a great day and another historic race.

CHAPTER TWENTY-THREE

When word reached Mendoza that Tango had won El Clásico El Ensayo with Isabella riding, she became more famous than the region's award-winning Malbec. The Mendoza Dog Rescue Center's website and voicemail in-boxes were flooded with inquiries about the grand opening of the center's rehabilitation facility, which was sure to draw a large crowd.

Amid the excitement, Carlos waited in the lobby of one of the most enchanting hotels in Mendoza, the Cavas Wine Lodge. Florencia slipped away to pick up an honored guest at the airport. Soon after, Carlos saw her walk into the lobby accompanied by a distinguished-looking man with long silver hair, dressed in a wine-red robe that fell just short of his ankles. Carlos could tell that the nut-brown-skinned man was from a faraway place, and somehow he could feel the tremendous inner strength the man carried in his peaceful and graceful manner.

"Carlos," Florencia said, taking his hand, "I would like for you to meet a very old and dear friend of Isabella's. This is Jamyang, from Tibet."

Carlos stood there, wide-eyed and speechless, as Jamyang smiled and bowed his head.

"Jamyang," Florencia said, "this is Carlos, the director of our new canine healing and rehabilitation program."

Carlos's skin tingled with goose bumps as he opened his arms to embrace Jamyang. "I cannot believe you are here in front of me. It truly is an honor. Without your great teachings and spiritual guidance, none of this would have been possible. We all must thank you. Isabella has honored you for so many years, and all the incredible stories we have heard of you and the gifts for healing have inspired her to pursue her passions. Today we will celebrate the miracles of the Dog Healers."

Jamyang smiled with pride. "Carlos, Isabella is the chosen one in the West. I knew from the first day we met, when she was a young child, that she would follow her heart and choose this path. Perhaps you might say that this path was predetermined, since she has always had an awe-inspiring connection with animals. For thousands of years, dogs have been man's devoted companions; they have an inner sense that guides them to heal our spirits and our souls. Isabella has what we call nature's divine guide, a free spirit to communicate and reciprocate with her heart and through the magic in the tones of her voice and the touch of her hands. I am honored to celebrate with you the grand opening of your center. As you know, I have not seen Isabella since she was a child, yet our spirits have remained connected from afar."

"After all these years she will be speechless when she sees you," Carlos told Jamyang. "Your presence will bring both tears and smiles and you could not have come at a better time. Please, after you get settled, I hope you will allow me to show you around our facility."

"Thank you all the same," replied Jamyang quietly, "but I have traveled many hours and I must get some rest."

Mark Winik

"Certainly," Carlos said. "Whenever you are ready, it would be my privilege."

Jamyang turned to Florencia. "Thank you so much for making all the arrangements to bring me here. The people in my village were excited that I was to travel more than halfway around the world. You honor me—and our tradition—with your generosity."

"Not at all," Florencia said as she warmly embraced Jamyang and kissed him on the cheek. "I am delighted that you were able to make this journey."

The following morning, Carlos and Jamyang met at the Cavas Lodge café.

"Buenos días." Carlos greeted his guest. "I hope you slept well and are rested. We have a full day ahead."

"I did have a restful sleep, until I was awoken by a nightmare."

"I am sorry to hear that."

"All I can remember from the dream is a small girl shivering in frigid conditions. She was digging a cave to protect herself from the cruel elements. She called out to me, from a distance, but I could not help her."

"It sounds frightening, but it was only a dream. The events in a dream usually don't happen in real life." Carlos tried to reassure him by changing the subject. "Jamyang, I am still in awe to have you here and very curious about your trip."

"Florencia sought me out. God knows how she was able to locate me. Since my parents and grandparents were trusted advisors to the Tibetan royal family, we were forced to flee the country. The Chinese military platoons desperately tried to capture us and a young holy man called the Karmapa. As we moved through the rugged mountain range avoiding capture, the many desperate platoons dwindled in great numbers. During this journey, the spirits of Mother Nature only blessed us, while they suffered the misfortunes of the wicked winds and the wrath of the frigid temperatures. The llamas and the chowstiffs gave us warmth, love, protection, and the strength to endure. To keep safe, we lived like Bedouins in the Himalayas and moved often between India, Nepal, and Bhutan. One day, a small group of Buddhist monks and a woman from India's foreign consulate appeared in our mountain village," Jamyang explained. "She said a very special woman from Argentina needed me to come to Mendoza, that she was fascinated by stories she heard of my life and my work with animals in Himalayas. She told me of her son's experience and his change in condition. She explained your center's mission, and how it would inspire and touch the lives of so many. I guess the thought of reuniting Isabella and me would be a great honor to both of us, and I am truly honored to see you carry the torch of healing spirits."

"Well, I cannot say enough how truly glad I am to meet you," Carlos responded. "We have learned so much from your teachings."

"I sense your knowledge and feel your devotion. You must celebrate and honor each living being that you and Isabella touch," Jamyang said, sipping his tea.

After Jamyang and Carlos left the café, they made their way to the Mendoza Dog Rescue Center where Carlos gave Jamyang a tour.

"We have a property of about five hundred hectares in total," Carlos said. "The land has been in our director Tamara's family for three generations. This property was once a large vineyard in Mendoza. Tamara's great grandfather came from Tuscany, Italy, to start an extension of the family's vineyard in the old country."

"The other portion of the land will be for our long-range plans, such as a camp for children with cancer, and areas where injured wild and domesticated animals can be cared for. Your teachings have helped us understand the mysteries of nature and just how important a role dogs and other animals play in lifting the human spirit and improving the healing process."

Carlos gestured toward one of the buildings. "In this building, we receive abandoned and abused dogs from all over," he said. "Our network of volunteers cares for the dogs and works hard at finding good homes for them. Please, let's take a walk to the rear of this building. This area is for socializing the dogs, especially the ones that have been abused. Over there is a forbidden zone; the fenced-in area has a tall, double-gauged steel fence around its perimeter. It's the dangerous Dogos' quarters. No one is allowed to step foot in it, or even touch the fence. The Dogos are the most vicious canines in South America. One of them nearly tore my limbs off. Thank God Isabella was there to help me."

"Dogos are no different from any other dogs; it's only their owners that make them dangerous. If you see them as one of your toughest challenges, I'm sure you and Isabella can help the Dogos overcome their vicious reputation," offered Jamyang.

Carlos wondered if Jamyang was right as he turned toward an adjacent building. "As you can see, this building has been entirely renovated and will be our new home for training people to heal the dogs using Kum Nye massage therapy. This is our pride and joy, and its existence has only been made possible thanks to the teachings you have shared with us."

"You know," Jamyang explained, "these healing techniques have been passed down for hundreds of years through my family. Generations of Tibetan teachers have shared their knowledge with no thought whatsoever of payment or benefit to themselves. It comes from their souls and is a gift that will now benefit so many more. It is heartwarming to hear that my ancestors' teachings made your work here possible, but how will you make certain that the people who adopt your dogs will treat them with respect?"

"The center requires that each person who adopts a Dogo go through our workshop program," Carlos explained. "The program reveals the many important facets of owning a dog and the responsibilities that come with ownership—establishing mutual respect.

"Our volunteers and trainers are each required to take the workshop. The first thing they learn is the magic that comes from a devoted dog's love. They learn that a dog understands a human's love and, in return, a dog intuitively cares for the human. Then, in turn, we urge all prospective new dog owners to also take the course.

"Jamyang, I learned to appreciate this as a result of my wonderful experience with Isabella, Roberto, and his dog, Moisés. We teach this philosophy and instruct our people in the power of touch and communicating with sweet, loving whispers. The dogs feel it and respond with appreciation. We call it our hands-on training—mending spirits with affection and touching tenderness through Kum Nye healing therapy.

"In the end, those who successfully complete the program proudly receive a certificate. In the past month, we've trained more than a dozen volunteers to coach the people who are adopting one of our dogs. In such a short time, our program has become a smashing success. The new dog owners and their dogs feel the love."

A wide smile spread across Jamyang's face. His eyes glistened as he indicated that they should join hands.

"I am filled with joy; you and Isabella have learned well. Please continue my family's ancient art of healing. It will change the lives of many and make the world a better place."

Carlos smiled as they embraced. He then led Jamyang in through the front door of the rehabilitation facility.

"Please, come inside," he said. He gestured to a space on the wall near the door. "This is our wall of fame for the training program. After we present participants with their certificates, we take a photo and put it on this wall. As you see, the people who complete our program are as proud to receive this certificate as they are to receive a diploma from a university. And notice the faces of the dogs; they are blessed with inner joy."

Jamyang nodded. "Yes, you can feel their smiles," he said.

"The feedback has been astonishing . . . so rewarding. And last but not least, here is our wall of healing stories. The first message was written by Florencia's son, Roberto, giving thanks to his faithful healing companion, Moisés. Roberto wrote, 'Moisés helped me through a time in my life when my doctors and my mother had given up. Moisés stayed by my side and cared for me in a way that no one could explain. He lifted my spirits and helped me through my suffering when I needed it most. Moisés is my magic, my healer, and my best friend forever and ever.'"

"You have built a wonderful facility and a program to be very proud of," Jamyang said. "But now I think you must get ready for all the guests."

"You're right. I lost track of time," Carlos said. "I must attend to the staff and today's program."

Just then, Carlos's cellphone rang. Isabella was calling from Santiago. "Hola, Carlos. I was calling to see how you are and how everything is going for today."

"Everything is fine, my dear. I can't believe you were Tango's jockey. What on earth happened?"

"Carlos, that story is for another time," Isabella said.

"Okay, well congratulations on your great victory. The grand lobby was packed with guests. It was so exciting and you and Tango were magnificent."

"Thank you, mi amor."

"Today is our big day."

"Indeed," Isabella agreed. "You must be busy."

"Yes, yes, there's still so much to do."

"Well, I'm at the airport and should leave shortly. We arrive in Mendoza in about an hour."

"I would love to meet you at the airport, but I have to be at the event. I will make sure someone picks you up. Have a safe flight, Isabella. Besitos."

"Besitos, mi amor."

CHAPTER TWENTY-FOUR

The pilot walked over to Isabella and said there would be a slight change in plans. The weather in certain parts of the Andes was showing strong winds with gusting downdrafts up to almost 100 kilometers per hour. "It could be dangerous to fly back to Mendoza in the small plane. It might be safer to fly by helicopter and navigate close through the peaks of the Andes," he explained.

Isabella shrugged her shoulders. "You're the pilot and I trust your judgment—as long as I can get back soon. I have an important event to attend."

"Thank you. Please, right this way; our helicopter is ready."

As soon as the pilot started the engine, Ricardo's cellphone rang. As he listened, a worried look spread across his face. He turned to Lucy and Isabella.

"I'm sorry, but an emergency has come up and I must fly straight to Brazil. Why don't the two of you go to Mendoza without me?"

"Ricardo, as much as I would like to attend our event in Mendoza, I think it's better that I be with you," she said. "You look stressed over the call."

"I agree, you should go with Ricardo," Isabella told Lucy. "He looks like he needs your help. Don't worry, I'll tell you all about the opening and I promise I won't leave out a thing."

Lucy looked at Isabella. "You know I wouldn't want to miss the event for the world."

"Don't feel guilty," Isabella said, giving Lucy a hug. "We'll catch up soon."

Isabella and Ricardo hugged and said their goodbyes. The pilot opened the door for Isabella and she quickly sat down and buckled her seatbelt. As soon as the door was latched, the pilot took off.

"The skies are clear but you never know what the weather will be like in the Andes," he explained without taking his eyes away from a vast collection of clouds moving swiftly through the sky. "We should be back in Mendoza in about forty-five minutes."

"I'm not good in the air and I'll feel much better when my feet touch the ground," Isabella said as she tried to relax. Indeed, it had been a busy weekend. Before she had a chance to relax, she suddenly jolted upright. "Oh, no!" she said.

"What's wrong?" asked the pilot.

"I forgot to call my brother."

"It's all right. Before you know it, we will be in Mendoza. Now please sit back, try to relax, and enjoy the scenic ride. You can call him as soon as we land."

"I guess so," Isabella replied.

Within fifteen minutes the helicopter was flying past the ice-covered peak of Tupungato, symbolic of the border crossing in the Andes. Isabella smiled, impressed by the ice- and snow-covered mountains as they passed between their jagged peaks. The steep slopes were so close you could almost touch them. The pilot constantly checked his control panel for safe passage. As they climbed a little higher in altitude, still hugging the mountains, the clouds below them turned dark and a strong gust tossed the helicopter from side to side.

Isabella grew uneasy. "What's going on?"

"Please try to relax; we just got caught in a crosswind. It is pretty typical," the pilot assured her.

CHAPTER TWENTY-FIVE

Back in Mendoza the sun was shining—perfect weather for an outdoor celebration. The staff, the volunteers, and the caterers were all prepared for the invited guests, who were due to arrive at any moment. The grounds were immaculate and the flowers were in full bloom.

Food and wine came from all over the region as a donation. Grill masters donated their time to feed the guests. The whole community was there to support the Mendoza Dog Rescue and Healing Center, as it was now called, in any way it could.

At eleven o'clock, Florencia and Tamara arrived with a group of dignitaries. Carlos made his way around the grounds, smiling at friends and ensuring that the guests were being attended to. Jamyang was given the honor of taking care of Roberto's dog, Moisés, and Isabella's dogs. It suited the self-contained Tibetan just fine and he was happy to do it.

Journalists and photographers had come to the event from all over South America. It was clear their interest centered on Isabella. Although they knew of her therapy work with dogs, the press, by and large, wanted the inside story about her riding Tango, and their unprecedented victory at El Clásico El Ensayo. No one seemed to know where she was. Noontime was approaching and Carlos was beginning to show signs of concern. He called her cellphone but it rang and rang with no answer.

Carlos and Florencia were anxiously awaiting her arrival while socializing with the guests. Suddenly, young Hector appeared and said, "Señor Guido Mondongo, the building inspector, wants to speak with you; he says it's very important."

"Oh no, what could he possibly want? I thought you took care of this with the mayor." He turned to Florencia.

"Well, I thought we did, but you never know. No worries, I can take care of him," Florencia replied. "Where is he, Hector?"

"Well, he is over that way. You can't miss him. He is short with a big belly and is wearing dark sunglasses, but please, señora, I will take you to him."

"Buenos días, Señora Florencia. It is a lovely day," Mondongo said while puffing on an expensive Cuban cigar. "I believe you have something for me, and you still need me to sign off on the approvals for your facility."

"Si, si, of course, Señor Mondongo, but can we do this in private?" Florencia replied.

"With pleasure," Mondongo said with a sinister-looking smile.

"Please follow me." She took them right past the Dogos' area. They watched Guido Mondongo with hungry eyes as they grit their teeth and growled.

Mondongo, unnerved by the vicious looks and sounds of the Dogos, said, "I hope their gates are locked tight."

"Well, these Dogos are typically friendly, but on occasion they have been known to leap over and attack, especially men whom they get a bad feeling about," Florencia noted.

"Well can we just take care of this? They are making me nervous," Mondongo said.

Florencia pulled a bulging white envelope from her leather-studded bag and handed it to Mondongo with a diplomatic smile. "I believe this is for you."

"Muchas gracias, señora. I hope it's all here," he said.

"Oh, I am sure it is, but please you should check it to see if it's correct."

Mondongo smiled with pleasure, opened the envelope—and pulled a handful of lascivious photos of himself and some naked women engaged in unsavory intimate acts.

"What the hell is this? This is blackmail."

"Oh, these are just copies and a token of our appreciation for our facilities' approvals. I particularly like this one," she said as she pulled out an original of the most obscene photo. I am sure your darling wife would also love this one. By the way, she looks absolutely stunning in her peach-colored linen dress today, and those pearls she is wearing must be very expensive. But please, I must get back to our guests. May I have the signed approvals? And once again, thank you for being a devoted public servant and giving your utmost support to our facility. That is, unless you want me to ask Hector to open the gates of the Dogos. Or, if you prefer, I would be happy to pass these most graphic images to your wife."

Guido Mondongo assented.

Florencia returned to the gala and smiled with an affirmative nod to Carlos. Carlos bit his lip and grew increasingly anxious. Isabella was scheduled to speak and give a presentation on Kum Nye healing therapy during the opening ceremony—and that was due to start at half past noon. Her arrival should have been some-time between eleven a.m. and noon, but she was nowhere to be found. Carlos tried to fight off the gnawing sense of discomfort.

Something was not right. She didn't call when she was supposed to have landed.

"Where is Isabella?" Florencia asked Carlos with a touch of agitation. "Have you heard from her?"

"I am beginning to think that she might have flown over the grounds, seen all the media vans, and said, 'No way,'" Carlos said with a mirthless laugh. "Perhaps she just wanted to avoid the whole scene. Yet this place means the world to her and I know she would never truly pass up the opening ceremony. I keep hoping she will call. I haven't heard a thing, nor has her brother Enzo, who is waiting at the landing strip."

"It's almost twelve-thirty, and Isabella is scheduled to speak," Florencia reminded Carlos, who was well aware of the schedule. "Carlos, what do you think? I mean, what should we do?"

Carlos took a deep breath. "We need to make some calls and see if anyone knows anything. Can you just charm the guests for a little while? It would be better than saying there has been a brief delay."

"Hey, I'm worried," Tamara whispered to Carlos and Florencia. "I hope she's all right."

"Well, let's just get started and hope that Isabella arrives soon," Carlos suggested.

The lights flashed. Tamara rose to the stage and called for everyone's attention. She welcomed the guests and thanked them for their support, offering hearty praise to the local and national dignitaries for their active participation in the Mendoza Dog Rescue and Healing Center's programs.

Tamara nodded to Carlos, and on his cue, twenty young volunteers walked out from the kennel area, each one with a dog on a leash. There were terriers and retrievers, mutts and Labradors, shorthairs and longhairs—dogs of all shapes and sizes. They strutted forward, wagging their tails with pride as they made their way to the stage. One at a time, the dogs were commanded to sit.

"These furry creatures are the real healers. They stand by us through thick and thin," Tamara told the crowd. The guests stood and offered a loud ovation.

After the applause died down, Tamara called some of the dignitaries onstage to be recognized for their contributions. They were the "who's who" of the dog world: the president of the South American Humane Society, the president of the South American Kennel Club, the president of Royal Canin, the premier dog food company in Argentina, the director of the Argentine Veterinary Association, and the head of a pet store chain. The young volunteers handed each dignitary one of the rescue dogs on a leash.

Veronica, the first of the young volunteers to receive a certificate, explained to the dignitaries that each of them had been assigned to a trainer who would guide them through the rudiments of the therapy program so they could experience the magic of Kum Nye healing massage therapy for themselves.

The dignitaries smiled as they experienced the hands-on demonstration, and the guests watched attentively. The press snapped picture after picture and recorded each moment. Veronica beamed as she walked up and down the stage, observing the reactions of the guests. She then turned to address the crowd.

Everybody applauded. Tamara took the microphone once more.

"As you can see, we have something extraordinary here. You may think it's our facility or our therapy programs, but I want to tell you what it really is. It is each one of these dogs that is special. They are the ones that deserve your applause." Everyone began to clap.

"No matter what age you are or how rich or poor you may be, whether you are sick or healthy," Tamara continued, "we are their caretakers, and the mission of our program is all about giving back to these devoted companions—with love, support, and Tibetan

Kum Nye healing. They deserve it, and it is our way of expressing our appreciation."

Tamara then introduced Carlos, "a man of great compassion, special talents, and a gentle way with dogs and people," as the new director of the Mendoza Dog Rescue and Healing Center. Amid thunderous applause and piercing whistles, Carlos walked up to the podium.

"I want to thank you for attending our grand opening," he said. "We are grateful to each and every one of you for finding a place in your heart to help support our mission to strengthen the bond between people and dogs, and to bring joy into the lives of all we touch.

"Today, we have a very special guest who has traveled here from the Himalayas in India, formerly of Tibet, to give us his blessing," Carlos continued. "Without him, we would not have such a wonderful program. Many years ago, Jamyang came to South America for a mountain trek up the Aconcagua, the highest peak in the Andes. At that time, he met a young girl and was captivated by her. She had a special gift and a gentle way to communicate with the animals. They were moved by her spirit. Jamyang knew she was the one in the West to receive the Tibetan ways of healing.

"That young girl was our beloved Isabella, the first Dog Healer in South America. Everything I have learned about healing animals, I've learned from Isabella. Ladies and gentleman, please welcome, from the peaks of the Himalayas, our guiding light and spirit of inspiration, Jamyang."

Jamyang slowly walked up to the podium. Tall and thin in stature, dressed in a long rose-colored robe that reached to his ankles, his spiritual presence radiated through the crowd before him. The dogs sat attentively with their respective dignitaries as if they knew the man before them was the soul of their spirit.

He looked at the dogs that sat with devoted attention and said, "These loving animals care for us like no other creatures on this earth. Today and everyday we need to give them our loving thanks. So please join me in a moment of whispering silence and feel the joy they give to us each and every day."

He took his hands from his heart and reached out to the dogs and then the audience to close their eyes and bow their heads in silent prayer and gratitude. For the next minute, there was complete silence.

Carlos continued with the program, and Isabella's brother Francisco made his way to the front of the crowd and approached Carlos at the podium. He grasped Carlos's arm, startling Carlos, who felt a shiver pass through his body. Francisco leaned over and whispered in his ear: "I have terrible news. Isabella's helicopter crashed somewhere in the Andes."

Carlos stared in disbelief, willing Francisco to take back his frightening words. Francisco, eyes brimming, clasped Carlos and said, "I can't believe it either." Both men, weak-legged, stood in shock.

Francisco's words sounded far away, but the look on his face made Carlos understand that the nightmare was real. Carlos began to tremble. Nervous and short of breath, he asked, "Did they find her or the helicopter? Is she alive? Please, can you tell me anything more?"

"I really don't know much," Francisco confessed. "Enzo phoned me from the airport to tell me the 'copter went down and that the Andes Mountain Patrol is sending a search-and-rescue team to find the pilot and Isabella, who was the only passenger."

Carlos nodded, collected himself as best he could, and asked why Ricardo and Lucy were not with Isabella. Francisco raised his hands in a helpless gesture and said he had no idea. "Isabella was supposed to call before she left to give us her ETA, but we never . . ." Francisco's voice broke and he could not go on.

Carlos felt sick to his stomach when he thought of Isabella as the sole passenger, knowing how she disliked flying under the best of circumstances. He couldn't bear the thought of how frightened Isabella must have been. He began thinking rationally about what had to be done. First, he eased his way closer to inform Tamara and Florencia of the tragic accident. They held on to each other for support.

Just then, Francisco's phone rang. "Hola?"

"Francisco, it's Captain Bruno. Our air patrol has located the helicopter. They think they spotted the pilot; it's a bloody mess. I am sorry to say there is no sign of Isabella, no emergency flares or any other distress signals."

"Where's the helicopter? Tell me exactly," demanded Francisco.

"It's in a deep narrow ravine, impossible for us to land, and the winds are so wicked, we can't even get close enough to drop a life stretcher. It is a dangerous situation. Our only option is to send a team of sled dogs. That's the only way in."

Francisco relayed the frightening news from Captain Bruno to Carlos. "Oh my God!" Carlos said, shaking with fear. "Can we get a helicopter? We have no time to spare. God help us, we need a miracle."

"Dear Lord," cried Tamara. "Is she alive?"

"I don't want to think about the worst," Carlos said emphatically. "Look, I have to go. You will have to figure out what to do with all these people."

Tamara pulled herself together, walked onto the stage, took the microphone, and asked for everyone's attention. "We have just received some frightening news," she said, still sniffling. "Isabella, our guiding light, was traveling in a helicopter that has gone down somewhere in the Andes."

A wave of gasps rolled through the audience. Isabella was the person that everyone had come to hear speak. Some of the guests were crying; others hugged their loved ones.

"Please, let us pray that the search-and-rescue mission is swift and successful," Tamara said. The guests and volunteers all bowed their heads while Tamara led them in a brief and heartfelt prayer.

The press moved into frenzy mode. The journalists and TV reporters were desperate to get any information about the crash. They volleyed to obtain any inside scoop from sources and gain any advantage they could about the accident. As terrible as it was, tragedy is always big news.

Enzo rushed to gather Carlos and Jamyang. "I secured a helicopter, and we will join the border patrol in the search-and-rescue mission. Please, every second counts. Gather up what we need and let's move," Enzo screamed in desperation.

"Please, we need a team of dogs that will know her scent," Jamyang said.

"In that case, any of the dogs that Isabella has worked with would know her scent," Carlos replied. "Take your pick. She's worked with almost all of them."

"You're right. Let's grab the dogs that have been closest to her."

Enzo rushed for Moisés and Isabella's own Malbec, who would stop at nothing to rescue her. Jamyang picked a couple of hearty huskies from the rescue center that could handle such extremely frigid conditions, and they proceeded to the helicopter that would transport the team. Francisco was already waiting with mountain gear.

CHAPTER TWENTY-SIX

While the pilot fired up the engines, Karina Romano—a reporter with TV12—signaled to Carlos and Jamyang to board the network's helicopter. Karina had been covering the ceremonies, but once she heard of the crash, she quickly sought and obtained clearance to use TV12's helicopter for the search-and-rescue mission; whatever the outcome, it would give Karina an exclusive story.

Carlos and Hector rushed the dogs toward the helicopter's open door. The dogs followed and intuitively leaped into the craft one by one. The last dog to come with Hector was Brutus, on a leash.

"What's he doing here?" Carlos snapped.

"I thought you wanted big, hearty dogs. I am just trying to help," Hector replied.

"Are you kidding me?" asked Carlos. "Brutus is as mean as any dog I have ever encountered! How did you even manage to get him to come along?"

"Isabella and I have secretly been working with him for a couple of weeks," Hector confessed. "I assure you, he is a new dog. Please take him with you. He adores Isabella and could be helpful."

"I don't believe this," Carlos said, sighing. He signaled to Brutus. "Come on boy. Let's find Isabella." Much to Carlos's surprise, Brutus stood patiently with his tail wagging as he joined the team.

"We're not equipped to have dogs on the helicopter! There are no seat belts for them!" the pilot shouted.

"The dogs will be fine," Jamyang reassured him. "I have done this many times. Please, let's move quickly. We have no time to spare."

"Okay—just keep them calm, especially for the takeoff."

The determined team flew off to meet Captain Bruno at the coordinates he had given them. Within thirty minutes, they came within range of the crash site—and hovered the craft just enough to survey it. Captain Bruno wasn't kidding when he said there was a bloody mess. It was impossible to access from the air, and their only choice was to find a flat, stable site on which to land, and then proceed on foot.

A few minutes later, they rendezvoused with Captain Bruno and his search-and-rescue team. The snow was deep—in some places waist high—which presented the dogs and the team with challenges, slowing their efforts.

"We're at an altitude of thirty-five hundred meters, so be very conscious of your movements," Bruno said, handing everyone a walkie-talkie. "The winds are blowing from the north at thirty-five kilometers per hour and the temperature is subzero. We just received a current report that a storm is moving in from the north. Trust me—this is a dangerous situation. My team is very skilled in these missions, and our protocol calls for sending one team right to the crash area while the other team searches for any survivors' movements away from the site.

"The helicopter may have had some type of engine failure or the strong winds may have forced it down. Since there appears to be no sign of an explosion at the site, I am optimistic, but few survivors have been known to endure such conditions for very long. There's no way to get a helicopter into the ravine without risk, so we must go in with dogs and experienced climbers," Captain Bruno explained.

"Our father taught us how to survive under the most extreme conditions," Enzo said. "If anyone has the strength and resources to survive, it would be my sister. She is strong willed, and God willing she survived the crash. I hate to think . . ." His voice trailed off.

Captain Bruno picked up on Enzo's thoughts. "If Isabella and the pilot survived the crash and were able to move, chances are they would seek refuge from the elements. In all likelihood, they would have left the craft, but we can't be sure where they would go or how far."

Bruno turned to Jamyang. "I gave Isabella this blanket to keep her warm as they were crossing the border through the mountains a day before El Ensayo," he said. "Take the blanket and give the dogs a whiff."

"Thank you," he said. "This should help." Jamyang put the dogs in their harnesses and gave them a good whiff of the blanket.

Carlos looked up at the leaden sky. "The storm front is moving in," he said. He turned to Jamyang and Enzo. "She could be anywhere if they survived and left the craft. Which direction should we go?"

Without a word, Jamyang removed the dogs' harnesses from the sled, hoping that one of them would pick up Isabella's scent so they could follow its lead. Once again, he placed the blanket near each dog's nose and then said to them in Tibetan, "Find your beloved healer."

The dogs scattered, each moving in a different direction to try to pick up the scent. There were only a couple of hours of daylight left, and the temperature was dropping with the setting sun. The wicked storm front fell upon them. Snowfall swirled around them as the wind picked up, making visibility near impossible. Carlos was shaking and shivering. He could barely feel himself, and had trouble breathing in such harsh temperatures, but he knew better than to lose heart. All he could focus on was finding Isabella and making sure that she was alive.

Ten minutes later, the dogs returned to the central site. Moisés, Isabella's dog Malbec, and Brutus were barking loudly. Carlos turned to Enzo and asked, "What is it?"

"Malbec must sense something, and now he is communicating with the other dogs," Enzo replied, feeling hopeful.

"I believe they are telling us they have picked up Isabella's scent," Jamyang added.

They quickly hooked the dogs back up to the sled. Carlos stood in the lead position and Jamyang stood behind on the sled's rungs as the dogs pulled them through the treacherous terrain. Enzo followed on snowshoes as rapidly as he could.

Along the way, Captain Bruno radioed Carlos. "We found the pilot! He's sustained some serious injuries and is nearly delirious; we are moving him with a rescue stretcher to the helicopter."

"What about Isabella?" Carlos shouted.

"No sign of her; the snow is falling too fast and there are no tracks in any direction," Captain Bruno told him.

"Well, where in God's country can she be?"

"The pilot could barely speak, but managed to let us know she survived and left the crash site to find a safe place and signal for help."

Carlos sighed with relief, but was still fearful since there was no sign of her.

Jamyang put a hand on his shoulder. "Her life is in the hands of the dogs," he said. "They know they are looking for her."

"How do they know?" asked Carlos.

"They know her scent from the blanket," Jamyang said. "She has a strong connection to them and they will do everything in their power to find her. After all, she is their healer."

—⊰⊱—

In the meantime, the news was broadcast over all the television networks and radio stations across South America:

> Following a terrible helicopter crash in the Andes, two rescue teams were assembled in a desperate search to locate the pilot and the beloved Isabella Borello, South America's most gifted horse trainer, who jockeyed Tango to victory at El Ensayo in Santiago, Chile. The pilot is reported to have been rescued and is in serious condition. However, as of this broadcast, there is still no sign of Isabella. The frigid conditions in the Andes are as wicked as anyone can imagine. All across South America, people are lighting candles and praying for Isabella's safety.

The troubling story was front-page news in every major city. In San Pablo, the headline read, "Still No Sign of Isabella." In Santiago, "Mountain Patrol Rescue Teams Are Hopeful." In Buenos Aires, "Isabella, Champion Horse Therapist, Lost in the Andes." In Bogotá, "Will the Champion Horse Trainer Survive?"

In Mendoza, the headline was more optimistic: "Therapy Dogs Determined to Find Their Healer."

CHAPTER TWENTY-SEVEN

Jamyang, Enzo, Carlos, and their team of dogs approached a steep slope, the first of many narrow ravines they would traverse. The moonlight was struggling to illuminate the night; its conflict with the blinding snowfall left the team at the mercy of Mother Nature. They prayed for the weather to subside.

Carlos stopped to catch his breath. He struggled with the high altitudes and subfreezing temperatures, but his emotions and adrenalin overcame the forces of nature and allowed him to keep going. He looked at Jamyang and Enzo, desperation visible in his eyes.

"How can she ever survive these conditions?" he asked.

"If anyone can, my sister will find a way," Enzo reassured him.

"I agree with Enzo," Jamyang said. "My dear friend Isabella's father was one of the most skilled Andes mountain guides. She and I spent much time together years ago when her father and I and a skilled team prepared for our mountain trek. Some of the lessons she learned from my teachings were about how to survive in the most severe conditions. She is strong and resourceful and she will remember those lessons, of that I am certain. Her great respect for nature and love for her animals will keep her strong and help her make it through the night. Trust me. The dogs will find her."

Carlos nodded, with tears frozen to his eyelids. He felt a bit more reassured by Jamyang's words, but it was still hard for him to imagine how Isabella could brave these harsh conditions and live to tell the tale.

The dogs were noticeably fatigued, but were intensely determined to continue their mission. Jamyang decided to free them from the sled and make camp for the night. Once he released the dogs, Moisés and Malbec took off, leaving only faint shadows in the wilderness.

"Moisés, Malbec, come back!" Carlos shouted.

"Let them go," Jamyang said. "Isabella's fate depends on them. They will not stop for anything until they locate her."

Carlos took a few deep breaths. Unable to face the idea that Isabella might be gone forever, the tears came. Brutus, who stayed behind with the men, recognized that Carlos pained deeply in his heart; he sidled up to him and began to lick his face. Despite his anguish, Carlos laughed a little as he remembered the day Brutus pinned him to the ground, daring him to move before nearly ripping his vicious jaws into him. The irony of his perceptions—he had once given up any hope for Brutus and forbade Isabella to work with him, and now he felt comforted by Brutus's loyalty and gestures of affection.

An hour passed. Carlos looked over at Enzo and Jamyang. "Any sign of the dogs?" he asked in an exhausted tone.

"Have faith in her dogs," Jamyang said gently. "They fully understand their purpose and will find her."

Moments later, Moisés wearily made his way through the deep drifts, panting breaths of exhaustion; he returned all alone, and Carlos panicked. "You're alone boy—where's Malbec?" he asked Moisés. There were no signs of Malbec as Carlos gazed with desperation through the blinding snowfall, with only his strong feelings of hope for a miracle. It was then, from a faint distance, that the excited tones of Malbec's bark could be heard through the violent winds. As Malbec got closer, his body turned in quick circles and his barking came louder and faster.

"Malbec wants us to follow him," Enzo uttered with a feeling of hope. "Detach the rescue toboggan. I think they've found her."

Carlos, Enzo, and Jamyang snapped their boots into snowshoes and followed behind all the dogs, who were barking with greater intensity. They struggled to lunge through the deep snow. Suddenly Brutus let out a series of whimpering cries.

"Where is he?" Enzo shouted.

"I don't know. I can barely see a thing," Carlos said.

Jamyang screamed, "Everyone, stop, don't make a move, you are standing next to an icy slope."

"Cast your flashlights in that direction." Jamyang pointed with his light.

"Enzo, get the bag with the climbing gear and pull out the ice picks with hooks, some rope, and carabiners. I think Brutus slid into the ravine," Jamyang said. "Now drive the ice picks into the ice with great caution," he instructed.

Jamyang secured the rope around his body and to the hooked ice pick, which was secured into the ice. He skillfully lowered himself into the ravine and cast his light in different directions.

"Do you see anything?" Carlos called.

"No, I see nothing but Ice and jagged rocks protruding through."

He cried out for Brutus and Isabella again and again. He heard only the echoes of his cries. Carlos felt distraught, and his hope quickly turned to fear. He felt betrayed by God—why were his prayers not answered? He collapsed to his knees and began crying hysterically, and when he exhausted his tears, at the top of his lungs he screamed to the heavens through the howling winds.

"Damn you, God! Why have you not answered my prayers? I am not a sinner; I have been a good man. Don't take Isabella and Brutus to your heavens. It's not their time. Please, God, I beg of you, send us a miracle." As he lifted his head and continued to cry out, the dogs felt his pain and snuggled close to him, and began to lick the wounds of his crying heart with their loving tongues for comfort.

Suddenly, the snowfall stopped, the winds subsided, and the full moon illuminated the surroundings. Malbec, Moisés, and the huskies, their scent no longer confused by the swirling winds, put their noses to the ground and began sniffing for Isabella. They scoured the area like a team of bloodhounds, suddenly moving in harmony through the snow, frantically barking.

Enzo shouted to Jamyang, "Please come, Jamyang! The dogs have picked up a scent again."

CHAPTER TWENTY-EIGHT

As Isabella peeked out of the shelter she had made and lit her last remaining distress flare, she heard the distinct sound of her dog Malbec barking in the distance. She would know his voice anywhere. Suddenly, Moisés came dashing over the frozen snow and dropped down, panting with excitement. His cries were like a song. He nestled himself close against Isabella's body to keep her warm. At first she thought it was a hallucination; after all, she had been stranded in the freezing cold for hours since the helicopter crashed. It was only when Malbec rushed into her shelter and licked her face that she realized these were not figments of her imagination, but the dogs she loved. They had come to her rescue.

Echoes of an unfamiliar voice again made her feel that this maybe surreal.

"Tenzin! Tenzin!"

She remembered the name given to her by Jamyang many years ago. Confused, she gasped at the voice from the distant past. She remembered Jamyang telling her that their spirits would transcend. Could this be real or was this the time when their spirits joined in the end? Was her mind muddled? She struggled to open her freezing eyelids; through the small opening of her shelter, she saw an old man peek in.

"Isabella, it's me, Jamyang."

Isabella still thought she might be hallucinating. Feeling light-headed, she crawled out of the shelter and stood teetering on her feet until she fell forward into Jamyang's arms.

"Oh my God, please let me touch you. Is this really you in the flesh? All I can remember is slipping on the ice and ending up in this ravine."

"Please save your strength." As he embraced her, his arms and body close against hers. "You must be dehydrated—sip some water. Your dogs picked up your scent and led us to you. Tenzin, you are weak."

Jamyang gently lowered Isabella's shaking body into a thermal blanket; her lips were blue, her eyelids were nearly frozen, and her skin was covered with patches of black. Her beloved dogs circled around her, lifted their heads to the heavens, and howled to the sky. Tears froze on her face as she hugged Jamyang and the dogs.

"It's a miracle—thank you, Lord."

"You survived, Tenzin, it's all right."

Jamyang yelled to Carlos and Enzo, "We got her! Isabella is very weak, but alive. Please lower the rescue toboggan!"

Jamyang carefully helped her into the thermal-lined toboggan and strapped her in. He guided the toboggan from below, while Enzo and Carlos hoisted her up the steep slope. Once they had pulled her to safety, Carlos broke into tears again. This time he said in a soft tone, "Thank you, God, for feeling my pain, and responding to my anger. Thank you for this miracle."

Carlos loosened the straps on the toboggan, and Isabella threw her arms around him, bursting into tears all over again as she hugged and kissed him.

Enzo, overjoyed to see his sister, gave her a huge hug. "I have never been so happy to see you," he said in a husky voice that was choked with emotion.

"I am still in shock; I can't believe that all the living souls closest to me are here. How on earth did you find me? Thank God we are all safe," Isabella said.

"Your beloved dogs were determined to find you, and there was nothing that could stop them. Isabella, we are sorry to say that we lost one of the dogs in the rescue," Enzo explained.

"Oh no, please don't tell me this is true. I can't bear the thought of losing any of them."

"The dogs worked all night together as a team. It was Brutus—he had the strongest connection to your scent and led the pack. All we remember is that his loud call to the others became more frequent, and suddenly, all we could hear were his cries, and then, only silence."

Isabella dropped her head and pounded the snow with her fists. "No, no," she cried. "God, don't take him! How I loved Brutus, he was my guardian angel and will forever be in my heart."

The other dogs climbed out of the ravine, raised their heads to the sky, and began to howl again, a sign of success and their call for celebration. They knew that Isabella was safe; the canine team had accomplished their mission.

"The winds are screaming again. The helicopter cannot land in these conditions, so we must move quickly and transport her to a more protected area, where we can set up camp for the remainder of the night," Jamyang told Carlos.

"I trust in your experience," Carlos answered, exhausted from the rescue, the storm, the altitude, and the relief of finding Isabella.

The frigid winds still sliced at the team as they made their way to safer ground. Enzo and Carlos erected their mountain tents. Once the shelters were completed, Jamyang escorted Isabella inside. He uncovered her hands and feet to increase warmth and improve circulation, then removed the rest of her clothes to treat her for hypothermia. Once he was satisfied that her condition was stable, he wrapped her in warm, thermal-lined clothes and let her rest. The dogs nestled close to her body.

In the morning, the sun made its chilly way through the mountain peaks, and the winds of the previous night subsided. Enzo radioed to Captain Bruno, alerting him that they had found Isabella, and asked him to send the rescue helicopter to land as close as possible to their position. Minutes later, the dogs began to bark; they heard the helicopter's engine in the distance. Jamyang reached into a bag and sent a burning flare into the sky.

Bruno landed first. As he stepped out of the helicopter, Carlos, Jamyang, and the animated dogs came over to greet him and his rescue team. Enzo stayed close to his sister.

"How is Isabella?" asked Captain Bruno.

"She is a lady of much inner strength," Jamyang said, "and her father would have been very proud of her today. His spirit shined on her, and all he taught her about survival skills, she used last night. This is how she survived through the night. I remember, when she was just a small child, her father was killed."

"Killed!" Carlos exclaimed. "She never mentioned a word to me about this."

"What do you mean, he was killed?" Bruno asked.

"He was a hero. He sacrificed his life to save his brother Freddo. It happened when we climbed the Aconcagua," Jamyang explained. "I remember he anticipated a fast-moving rock and ice slide from above. He had such keen instincts—he released himself from his harness, and when he swung around, he pushed his brother to safety. His foot got stuck in a crevice, and it was too late. Her mother passed within a year of his death."

"Life presents us with many obstacles to overcome, and sacred memories, some of which we keep in our hearts and dare not share. But our shared love for animals has reunited us in the

Andes, closer to the heavens, the blessed place where her father passed," said Jamyang.

"Wow, I had no idea. She has been through a lot," Bruno said. "Thank God that the dogs she loves and her friends and family have rescued her."

Carlos, shaken by Jamyang's revelations, extended his hands to the wise healer. "Thank you for enlightening me, and for your devotion to Isabella."

Bruno left the two men alone, walked over to the last standing tent, and poked his head through the entrance. "How are you feeling, my dear?"

"I just can't believe it." She wept. "My brother, my dogs, my teacher, and the love of my life have rescued me. And now you— you have saved me twice. I cannot tell you how grateful I am to you, Captain."

"I hope we don't need your rescue services again," Enzo said to Bruno, smiling.

Bruno laughed. "I hope the two of you will stay safe from now on," he told Enzo, then turned back to Isabella. "You are incredible. I don't know how you survived this accident and the extreme conditions of the unforgiving Andes. Many have not. But please don't thank me. From what I hear, you must thank these heroic animals. In all my years I've never experienced as challenging a search-and-rescue mission as this one. We could never have done this without the help of these brave dogs.

"Please, I want you to have this as a keepsake; it's the blanket I gave you at the border crossing. This saved your life; the dogs used it to pick up your scent. And one more thing, my dear: Congratulations on your victory at El Ensayo. You made me a bundle, and I hope you don't mind that we may have helped change the odds a little."

Isabella stopped crying and looked perplexed. "What do you mean?" she asked.

"The other trainers at El Ensayo heard that Tango's muscles had sustained some injuries from the cold the night before in the Andes," Bruno said with a wink. "They *heard*."

Isabella smiled at Bruno. "You're such a devil," she said, her eyes crinkling. "Don't worry; it's our little secret."

CHAPTER TWENTY-NINE

K arina and the crew from TV12 rushed out of their chopper to record the heroic rescue. As the cameraman zoomed in on the dogs, they lifted their heads to the sky and, like a pack of wolves in the wild, let out an endless concerto of howls, alerting the world that their rescue was successful and that Isabella was safe.

Suddenly, the sounds of a whimpering animal could be heard in the distance. Isabella and Carlos looked around. It was a bit of a blur, blending with snow, but they could make out a large white animal struggling toward them. He moved as though he was injured.

Carlos looked closer and yelled, "Oh my God!"

"What is it?" Isabella said.

"It's a miracle, that's what it is. It's Brutus. He's alive."

Brutus wearily leaped toward Isabella, barking frantically with each push. Isabella felt shivers migrate through her body, and rushed to meet Brutus. So thrilled when they connected, he jumped, and the two fell into the snow. Brutus cried with joy and licked her face over and over.

"Oh my God, I can't believe it!" The two frolicked in the snow. "Thank you for risking your life, and thank you for being alive!"

Brutus smiled up at her and wagged his tail.

Karina looked straight into the TV camera with watery eyes, microphone in hand, ready to share the story.

"After a frightening helicopter crash in the Andes, and amid some of the most horrific weather conditions we can imagine, this heroic and devoted team of dogs relentlessly searched through the night— without food or sleep—to find Isabella.

"Our beloved Isabella—known to all as the Dog Healer—survived the accident and the night against all odds. She attributes her survival to all that she learned from her father, and from her lifelong friend, a Sherpa from the majestic Himalayan mountains in Tibet.

"Before the Argentine border patrol's EMS team transports her to her home in Mendoza, let's see how she's doing." The reporter approached Isabella, microphone in hand. "How on earth did you survive?"

Isabella turned to the camera. "I am the luckiest woman alive," she said. "I want to give my special thanks to Captain Bruno and the Andes Mountain Patrol team, my teacher Jamyang, my beloved Carlos, my wonderful brother Enzo, and my truly amazing dogs. The world should know that these loving animals have given my life's passion great meaning."

"All right!" bellowed Captain Bruno. "Time to move on."

The two helicopters started their engines to complete their mission and journey back to Mendoza.

Soon, every television and radio station in South America bombarded the airwaves with reports of one of the most dramatic rescues in the Andes. Stories about the rescue were heard around the world, followed by stories about the Mendoza Dog Rescue and Healing Center and its innovative programs.

In the coming weeks, people sent heartwarming stories about their own dogs—and miracles—in thirty different languages, addressed to the Mendoza Dog Rescue and Healing Center or directly to Isabella in care of the center. They shared their tears and their joys and wrote about the dogs that lifted their spirits each day and healed them when they needed it most. Unsolicited donations poured in from all over and funded the center to support its programs for many years.

CHAPTER THIRTY

Sipping my cappuccino at Cafe Martinez, and lost in time, I looked at Carlos, astounded by the turns his story had taken. Isabella's life story was filled with many obstacles to overcome, dreams to pursue, and spirits to touch. This truly inspiring journey helped me look at life with a new meaning, an enlightened perspective, and now I understand what he meant when he said that he had met a woman that changed his life forever.

"This is an incredible story," I told him, "and now I understand why you're the most respected Dog Healer in Buenos Aires. But I'm still curious how you ended up back here. I thought you were the director of the center in Mendoza?"

"Yes, Marco, I was the director of the center, and after the dust settled from Isabella's rescue, I stayed on as director. Our growth was explosive. We rescued and placed more dogs than any other facility in South America. People came from all over to attend our programs and become certified in our techniques. We started our camp and therapy outreach program and those, too, were immensely successful. Trainers, groomers, veterinarians, breeders, and other rescue centers wanted to learn and offer our methods.

"As director of the center in Mendoza, my life was stressful. I longed for a simpler lifestyle. My mother needed help, so I returned. Señora Solas was kind enough to introduce me to her friends and their beloved dogs. Every few months, I give a workshop to dog lovers from all over the world. They come to learn the principles of Kum Nye healing and massage. In fact, I just received an interesting text from one of my more motivated students. He is giving workshops around the United States, which he features as 'Scrassaging' the Dog."

"Amazing," I said, aware that I was repeating myself. "Just amazing. You are truly blessed. But I have one more question: Whatever became of you and Isabella?"

Carlos smiled. "Jamyang once told Isabella that if she followed her passions, her dreams would be fulfilled. She and Malbec travel the world as ambassadors for the center, and teach of the wonderful bond that humans and dogs share together.

"What can I say? I can still feel the passion of her lips from our first kiss at Echo's Peak. Our hearts grow like flames of a fire and the flames are like an endless torch that keeps burning, whether we are together or apart.

"Mi amigo, I hope you will come to our wedding celebration. But please, it will be dark soon. We still have a few dogs to return."

ACKNOWLEDGMENTS

I want to thank the people that helped inspire and support this creative endeavor:

Storyline consultant: Rachel Bergman
Copyeditor: Dennis Ambrose
Photograph and graphics: Lisa Nichols
Graphic design: Gil Hokayma
Model: Marah Nichols
Author photograph: Chad Lyons

Dog Healers supporters:

Len Mirto, Jennifer Dewitt, Dean Stearman, Lesley Roy
Mitch Young, Cheryl Maturo, Bob Wolinsky
Dennis Weiner, Mendy Hecht, Ian Gottleib, Sandman law group
Willard Finkle, Mendy Katz, the Bennun family
Harvey and Nancy Gottlieb

To all the great organizations, rescue and canine therapy groups, and their volunteers:

Pet Partners, ASPCA, Humane Society
Angels on a Leash, North Shore Animal League America
Cosgrove Animal Shelter, Woofstock, Dog 4 Warriors
Best Friends Animal Society, Petsmart Foundation, Petco Foundation
HSUS/Friends of Finn, Rescue Me, Animal Rescue, Paws with a Cause
ASDA, Guide Dogs of America, DogWish.org, Canines 4 Hope
Guiding Eyes, Pawsitiveservice dogs, Fidelco.org
Cesar Millan Foundation
and the many others that dedicate their support

ABOUT THE AUTHOR

Mark Winik, an avid dog lover, lives in Short Beach, Connecticut, with his wife, Norma, and their two dogs. On any given day, you'll find Winik advocating for dogs, participating in community events to benefit animals, and encouraging others to get involved. He founded a dog park in Branford, Connecticut, a valuable resource for the dog-loving community, and a testament to Winik's own devotion to our furry friends.

On a visit to Buenos Aires, his wife's home city, he discovered Carlos DeMarco, the Dog Healer. This profound experience inspired Winik to write this incredible story.

Facebook.com/thedoghealers
thedoghealers.com
@TheDogHealers
Instagram.com/thedoghealers